The Ballantine Reader's Circle Reader

BALLANTINE BOOKS · NEW YORK

A Ballantine Book
Published by The Ballantine Publishing Group

http://www.randomhouse.com/BB/
http://www.randomhouse.com/BB/readerscircle

Manufactured in the United States of America

First Edition: April 1999
10 9 8 7 6 5 4 3 2 1

CONTENTS

April 1999

May 1999

June 1999

July 1999

August 1999

September 1999

November 1999

The Ballantine Reader's Circle features quality trade paperback fiction from critically acclaimed bestselling authors with discussion guides bound into the back of the books themselves. All guides include unique interviews with the books' authors—Connie May Fowler, Mary Doria Russell, and Louis Begley, to name a few. To recognize a Ballantine Reader's Circle title, look for the distinctive circle logo on the front and back covers as well as the spine.

THE READER

Since its start, the Ballantine Reader's Circle has been a tremendous success. So to celebrate 1999, a year featuring still more remarkable authors, we're offering this reader, a unique original trade paperback to introduce reading groups to more wonderful characters. Eighteen acclaimed authors have contributed selections of their works available as Ballantine Reader's Circle titles. Each of their editors have also written a personal introduction describing what delights them about their authors' fiction. Naturally, we hope you find all of these selections satisfying, but we suspect you'll fall in love with at least a few of these characters and want to share them with your reading group. For you and your reading group, we've included a complete listing of resources and new features in the back of this reader. *And* you'll also find a special contest offer—because we'd love to hear all about your reading group experience. Enjoy and good luck!

THE ALL-TRUE TRAVELS AND ADVENTURES OF LIDIE NEWTON

Jane Smiley

Dear BRC Reader,

Jane Smiley is a writer of extraordinary range, a Pulitzer Prize–winning novelist, whose every new novel is different from the one before it, and each superb. Among her previous works: a suspense novel, *Duplicate Keys*; contemporary novellas and short stories, *The Age of Grief* and *Ordinary Love and Good Will*; a fourteenth-century saga, *The Greenlanders*; the great tragic novel, *A Thousand Acres*, which won the Pulitzer Prize; and an enchanting comedy, *Moo*.

The All-True Travels and Adventures of Lidie Newton, set in the 1850s, speaks to us in a splendidly quirky voice—the strong, wry, nononsense voice of Lidie Harkness of Quincy, Illinois, a young woman of courage, good sense, and good heart who impulsively marries, then falls deeply in love with Thomas Newton, an abolitionist from Boston, as he passes through Quincy on his way to Kansas where he intends to settle, hoping to help assure the entry of Kansas into the Union as a free state. Plain and headstrong—she rides and shoots and speaks her mind—Lidie seems born for pioneer life. This is her story—a woman in a fiercely male world who triumphs in the midst of adversity and discovers herself.

Leona Nevler
Senior Vice-President
and Editorial Director

I Become Acquainted with Mr. Thomas Newton

Wash the fine clothes in one tub of suds; and throw them, when wrung, into another. Then wash them, in the second suds, turning them wrong side out. Put them in the boiling-bag, and boil them in strong suds, for half an hour, and not much more. Move them, while boiling, with the clothes-stick. Take them out of the boiling-bag, and put them into a tub of water, and rub the dirtiest places, again, if need be. Throw them into the rinsing-water, and then wring them out, and put them into the blueing-water. Put the articles to be stiffened, into a clothes-basket, by themselves, and, just before hanging out, dip them in starch, clapping it in, so as to have them equally stiff, in all parts. Hang white clothes in the sun, and colored ones, (wrong side out,) in the shade. Fasten them with clothes-pins. Then wash the coarser white articles, in the same manner.—p. 286.

Thomas Newton was what Harriet's husband, Roland Brereton, called a "d—— abolitionist." So was our sister Miriam. Roland Brereton called her "your d—— abolitionist sister Miriam." Roland was forever d——ing everything, even those things he was fond of, like his dogs and his horses. Roland was from Kentucky; he and his three brothers had moved across the Ohio River into Illinois when Roland was a small boy. Roland's family had gotten entangled in an Illinois legend almost as soon as they set foot in the state, and all the old settlers knew who the Breretons were.

The story runs as follows. There once was a family of killers who lived down near the Ohio: an old man, his four sons, and the women who might have been their "wives." They lived in the woods in a primitive fashion, making camps at night and taking shelter as best they could. It was said by reliable authorities that the women took the babies away from the camp every night to sleep, because they knew that if a baby cried, the old man would kill it. To meet up with these men was almost certain death. Many men of that day were lost and never heard of again until their bodies were found. One man was caught and tied to his horse. The horse and the man were blindfolded, and then the horse was driven over a high bluff. Another time, a group of pioneers got separated from two of their children, as it was easy to do in those days, and when they found the children, a day later, it was only to discover that they had been run down and brutally murdered for the sake of stealing what little clothing they were wearing. This father and sons were said to have killed over a hundred men, women, and children in two years or so, and heaven knows how many before they came to Illinois.

Roland Brereton's father, Lyman, came into Illinois from Kentucky right at the time when all of these killings were taking place, and sure enough, one evening, when they were pushing their way along a woodland track down in Edwards County, three men, one old and two young, jumped up in front of them, far gone in drink but deadly. Lyman was walking along at the horse's head, Roland and his two brothers were in the wagon. The mother was behind the wagon, and their dog, some sort of Kentucky hound dog, was walking next to her. As soon as the three men approached, the dog slunk away.

The brutes were greedy, and they paused to rummage through the Breretons' belongings, though they didn't pause long. Any object was good enough for them to kill for. But the dog had made good use of this moment to seek out Burton Brereton, Lyman's brother, who was some yards ahead of the group. Burton was one of those Kentuckians who seemed to take after red Indians rather than his white ancestors, and he was there before they even heard him coming. The only one of all of them who saw him was the mother, and what she saw was Burton setting the muzzle of his long rifle against the back of one of the sons' heads and pulling the trigger. At the very moment of the shot, she called out, "Praise the Lord!" at the top of her lungs. The old man and the other son got away and lived to kill other pioneers, but the Breretons got famous all the same for at least reducing their number.

For all that, Lyman and Burton Brereton didn't make much of a success in Illinois. According to Roland, they didn't have any use for good prairie soil and stuck to little patches here and there in the woods. Like most Kentuckians, they were satisfied to shoot something for supper and have some greens with it. But Roland had made himself a nice prairie farm out east of Quincy, and the only Kentucky left in him was the everlasting d——ing of this and that, and the dogs that over-ran the place, all said to be descendants of the famous hound that saved the family. Roland wouldn't have a slave, not even in the kitchen, but he'd die for the right of all his second and third cousins that he'd never met to own as many slaves as they wanted. I doubted he'd be called upon to offer his life, unless he died as a result of an apoplectic fit after a dispute with some d—— abolitionist. But abolitionists weren't all that common in Quincy, though there were some who sympathized with "poor Dr. Eels," as Beatrice called him, who'd tried to rescue an escaped slave who'd swum from the Missouri side, back when I was a little girl, and had been convicted on account of the wet clothes that were discovered in his buggy. Most people in Quincy didn't go out of their way to help the swimmers from Missouri, but they didn't go out of their way to return them across the river, either. My brother-in-law Horace once said, "My opinion is, it's a pretty short swim over but a pretty long row back, and I just don't want to make the effort." That was Quincy all over.

I found Thomas Newton much milder and quieter than you'd think a "d—— abolitionist" would be. He was so mild and quiet, in fact, that the first time I met him, when he came over to Harriet's in the company of the neighbor Howell, who was also a d—— abolitionist, I didn't find out a thing about him. I was out at Harriet's helping her boil bed linens about two weeks after my father's funeral. I was trying to be as little use as I could be, but I could hardly fail to stir the boiling clothes, my assigned labor. It was a hot day, and I had tied up my skirts to keep them out of the fire and rolled up my sleeves to keep them out of my way. My hair was so heavy with damp from the work that it hung around my shoulders. Harriet's boy Frank was tending the fire. Howell drove up in his wagon, and he and a tall fellow with pale hair and fair skin got out and went into the house. I can't say that I made much of him. There was a creek down behind Roland Brereton's farm, and I was thinking mostly about taking a swim back there if I could slip away from Harriet after the clothes were washed.

But Harriet was thinking about something else, and not three minutes after Howell and this pale fellow went into the house, they came out again, with Harriet right behind them, and she had a tray in her hand and on that a jug of cold spring water. Pretty soon, she set them up on a cloth in the shade of a big hickory tree, went back in for glasses and a plate of cakes, and then she sang out to me, "Lidie! Surely those linens are clean by now. You better fix yourself up and come over here and have a glass of water in this heat! Isn't it sweltering!" And the two men made themselves comfortable, all smiles.

This neighbor, Roger Howell, hadn't owned his farm long. He'd come down from Wisconsin, along the bluffs of the Mississippi, and was said to be consumptive, which was why he found the winters up there too much to bear. He had gingery whiskers and a bald head with a gingery fringe around the sides, and he was always taking his hat off and putting it on. Harriet told me that every night he smeared on his pate a mixture of hartshorn and oil, which Jonas Silk swore would grow hair on a stone, but no new shoots were as yet in evidence. The only thing I'd ever heard him talk about was his mare, which he was very proud of—he'd won her in a poker game from a Missouri man, and she was a long-legged, haughty-looking thing with a white circle around her left eye and a wide blaze.

"Well, Tom," he was saying as I came up, "you were impressed. I saw you holding your hat, but that mare wasn't even stretching out. On the one piece, that straightaway before you get to the gate here, she whipped Solomon Johnson's colt, hardly even breathing. Broke that colt's heart—"

Thomas Newton started to stand up, but I sat down so quickly on the cloth that he didn't have a chance. Harriet pushed a glass of water over to me and beamed on me as if I were her dearest child, while at the same time shooing away Frank, who was twelve at the time. "Yes, Mr. Newton, here is my sister, my baby sister Lydia, the last of us girls. Do you know, my father had thirteen daughters altogether?" She motioned to me to straighten my bodice and otherwise surreptitiously rearrange myself, but it was too hot for that. I sat down as I was. "Good land," Harriet went on. "It's miserable weather for boiling clothes, but Lidie simply would do it. There was nothing I could do to stop her."

Howell remarked, "My mare don't notice the heat. She hardly

turns a hair in this heat. Tom Newton, you ever seen a mare like this one? I swear!"

Frank stood opposite us, under the hickory tree, with his thumbs notched in his braces.

Now Thomas Newton spoke for the first time. His voice was low and agreeable. "You know I'm not a horseman, Howell. And you weren't, either, the last time I saw you. You've been transformed by this Missouri mare!"

Howell grinned at this as if it were praise. Harriet grinned to be agreeable. Howell said, "Now look at her just stand there. She—"

"Miss Harkness, are you fond of horses?"

"When there's one to be fond of I am."

"Lidie's just a miracle worker with dumb creatures," said Harriet. "More of our delicious spring water, Mr. Newton? Will you be with us long?"

Very slowly and with much aplomb, Frank pulled the stub of a seegar from his pocket and put it between his lips. A moment later, he pulled out a lucifer and lit it. He sucked through it and then let the smoke pillow out of his mouth. Harriet, I could see, was trying to ignore him. Mr. Howell seemed to be ignoring him, too, except that he turned suddenly and spat a thin brown stream toward the woods. Thomas Newton, it appeared, neither smoked nor chewed.

I came to realize that this is what my sisters had decided on, marrying me off to the first stranger to pass through Quincy, or the second, or the third.

He said, "Only as long as I can help it . . ."

"Tom Newton's on his way to Kansas," said Howell. "He's with the Massachusetts Emigrant Aid Company. Roland around?" Now Howell grinned again. "I do want to make sure that Roland meets Tom. I know he'll want to."

"My goodness me," said Harriet. "You mean you want to give him a fit! Are you an argumentative man, Mr. Newton?"

"He's from Boston, an't he?" said Howell, laughing aloud.

"Let me suggest, sir," said Harriet soberly, "that you refrain from engaging Mr. Brereton in discussion if you find him armed."

"He's always armed," said Howell.

Harriet nodded at this, as if to say, There, you see.

Howell roared, "He's itching to kill some d—— abolitionist!"

Thomas Newton paled and quickly took a sip of his water. Howell shouted, "Here he comes now!" and Harriet started and looked around, and Thomas Newton kind of hunched into himself, but Howell was laughing to beat the band, pleased to have made fools of us. I finished my glass and stood up, ready enough to get back to stirring the clothes, but Harriet said immediately, "Lidie, pass Mr. Newton one of these cakes you made yesterday," and what could I do? I passed the cakes, which I had never seen before, and they began to slide off the plate, and he didn't have the sense to catch them, so they all fell in his lap. A hapless young man, that much was clear.

Frank fell over laughing.

Harriet seemed to place the blame on me. She exclaimed, "Oh, Lidie, for goodness' sake!" Howell was laughing, too, but I got up without glancing at Mr. Newton and went back to stirring my clothes, which heaved and billowed in the steaming waters. It seemed the most harmless thing I could do.

Soon enough the bald-pated older man and the pale young man got into the gig and went off, and not long after that, Harriet, with a distinct air of disappointment married to long-suffering resignation, declared that she was going to her room—"because, Frank, you have given me a headache with that infernal cheroot"—and after we were finished with the rinsing, would we leave the clothes to sit in the bluing tub, and so we did, Frank pausing twice to relight his seegar, because, taken all in all, he wasn't nearly as experienced with it as he liked us to think.

The stream below Roland Brereton's farm cut down its banks in muddy steps and in spots you could stand in the middle of the stream and see only the sky and tufts of thick grass edging the banks high above your head. By late afternoon, there were two shady spots, cool under the giant cottonwoods, and at one of these Frank had dammed a little pool that in mid-August ran about a foot deep, deep enough for bullheads, sunfish, a crappie or two, and, of course, numerous scuttling crawdads. The small terraces that defined the height of the waters in earlier periods of the year were dried and cracked into an gular shapes. Frank liked to pluck the little squares out of the mud and spin them into the pool, or follow the crawdads with a stick and poke after them into their hiding places. A few late rays of sunshine through the cottonwood leaves fell on the muddy water and sparkled, but without disturbing the sense of cool shade and privacy that I always felt in this spot. I could hear Roland's cows lowing in the pasture above us, but the banks of the creek were too steep for them until some quarter of a mile downstream. Often, we saw turtles in the water, snakes, which held no fear for me, and the tracks of coons and skunks in the mud. The banks had a number of otter holes, and a ways upstream the otters had made a slide, but we didn't often see the otters themselves, unless it was the flash of a rounded little head accompanied by the sense of being looked at with sharp, black little eyes, and then, as soon as you turned toward them, they were gone. The creek had a different, more solitary and less appalling, feeling than the big river, which I also frequented. The high banks and tall trees gave it the almost domestic air of a dwelling place. Of course, I resorted to it far more often than Harriet thought proper for a young woman of my station.

But in fact, my station was clearly low and dipping lower.

Though he died owning a house, my father hadn't made much of himself either in Ohio, where he'd gone after marrying Ella and where he'd met my mother, or in Quincy, where he had brought his many daughters to marry them off around the time I was born. He had no knack for farming—preferred a more convivial life than that, with theatricals and clubs and levees and daily social intercourse. Some years, he would broker some grain down the river or some cotton up; other years, he would have an interest in some dry goods or some horses to sell. The lot where he built his house came to him through a trade—a German man owned the lot but needed a quantity of barley to make beer, and my father happened to have an interest in a quantity of barley. The house itself got built in the same way, and it was a house with a pleasant air about it, because my father liked to make a good appearance above all things. But he was sixty-two when I was born, and the novelty of daughters had worn away long before.

My mother doted upon me—perhaps not so much at first, but more as I lived longer and longer and proved myself healthier and less likely to follow my mother's other babies to the grave week by week and month by month. By the time I was four and had outlived them all, I could do no wrong in her eyes, nor could she do any wrong in mine. I was a good-tempered child, for I had my own way in everything, and she poured out on me all the love and attention she had stopped up over the years. I knew my letters at two, could read a newspaper and do sums at four, tell stories from the family Bible at five. She found me other books, with no discrimination of judgment or taste. It so pleased her to hear me read that she would listen to me read anything, thinking, perhaps, that the matter of the reading simply ran through me like water through a spigot. She sewed for me and tatted for me and cooked me special dishes, persuaded my father to procure me a pony, and altogether we lived like a potentate and her adoring servant, and it was a fine life for me, my delight and my due. But she was a shy woman and had few friends. Perhaps we were such friends to each other that she felt she needed no one else. And then there were Miriam, Beatrice, Alice, and Harriet, making their usual noise. That might have been enough for her. When I was thirteen, the cholera came up the river, and of all of us, only my mother took ill. She died within three days. She was forty-seven.

This time, my father, who was seventy-six, didn't look around for a new wife, only for some place to put me, and that is how I went to Alice's, where I was hardly a potentate but only one of many, and there I discovered my taste for that sort of freedom, the freedom of not being attended to. To my old bad habits of indiscriminate reading and stating my opinion whenever I desired to, I added new ones of wandering about, spending time at the river, avoiding housework, and improving my fishing and hunting skills with the help of Alice's many sons. But I cannot say that Alice or her husband, Frederick, who had a small lumbering mill, or any of their sons was blessed with connections, either, so Harriet's notion of my station was largely a fiction.

Frank said, "I got some money."

This was hardly unusual, as Frank was an enterprising young man, who, moreover, was as much master of his own time as any boy twice his age. I said, "How much do you have?"

"Four dollars."

Four dollars, on the other hand, was a considerable sum, suspicious in a boy.

"How'd you get that?"

"I only get to keep four bits. But I got it here in my pocket."

"How'd you get it, I asked you."

"Mr. Thomas Newton gave it to me. He told me to take it. You want to come with me?"

I didn't answer anything, but he started walking down the creek, keeping in the middle and careful, I quickly saw, to refrain from stepping in any muddy spots. Frank pulled out the last of his seegar and stuck it between his lips, but he didn't light it. We didn't say anything. We passed the lower banks of the cow pasture, but the cows couldn't be seen from the creek. Everything was quiet. We kept going until we came to a small cave, a spot that I knew Frank had explored extensively. We stopped, and Frank looked eagerly in. I did not. I could hear well enough: movements of some large body, audible only when they suddenly were stilled. I knew there would be a dark face in there. I didn't have to see it. Frank picked up some stones by the creekside and heaved them idly into the water, the way a boy would do, aiming at this snag or that one. Then we walked on until we got to the next cow pasture, where we came up out of the creek and paused to pick mulberries. I said, "Well?"

And he said, "I left it under a rock."

"Did anyone see you?"

"Only the one that was supposed to see me."

We carried the mulberries home in Frank's cap. Mulberries are funny. Most of the time they don't taste like a thing, but these were sweet as could be. Harriet didn't know whether to be pleased with the mulberries or angry at the stains all over our faces and hands. It was my responsibility to admonish him, she declared. But the fact was, I always seemed to let Frank do just what he pleased.

© ROBERT BLAKEMAN

JANE SMILEY is the author of eight previous works of fiction, including *The Age of Grief*, *The Greenlanders*, *Ordinary Love & Good Will*, *A Thousand Acres*, which won the Pulitzer prize, and *Moo*. She lives in northern California.

THE MIRROR

Lynn Freed

Dear BRC Reader,

The Mirror is unlike other novels taking place in the first half of the century in that at its core is a truly modern, feminist woman—a woman not afraid to pursue her own desires or to embrace her unique strength and power. At a time when most women found their identity as wives and mothers, Agnes was unapologetically unimpressed by both. She found her husband and her child's needs a hindrance to her own, and despite their wishes, lived her life according to her own rules and standards. Decades before her time, Agnes unabashedly explores her sexuality and relentlessly pursues securing a stable life for herself without the aid of a man. We picked this novel for our list because the themes Freed so stunningly presents are ones that every generation of women must face. Within Agnes's intriguingly honest, unsentimental story, all women can find a trace of themselves.

In this excerpt, Agnes chronicles the trip she takes to the countryside to visit her lover of five years, a sailor who is also her friend Constance's first love. When her husband finds an unsent love letter to the sailor, the two engage in a furious argument resulting in Agnes's decision to be dictated only by her own conviction. Despite the hysterical protestation of her young daughter Leah and the silent outrage of her husband, Agnes sets off on her journey. This is a pivotal moment in her life, for she realizes that to move forward, to do exactly what she wants, she must always leave something behind.

Sarah Glazar
Assistant Editor

It was a tiring journey, three days in the heat switching and changing and showing my papers for stamping. But it was lovely, too, stopping at the little towns, and then the plains of yellow grass and the umbrella trees, and the mountains blue in the distance. After a while, there were even animals to see—zebras and antelopes and giraffes with their babies, all looking up as we passed as if we were interrupting their tea. And every now and then the native children would come running from their kraals and dance next to the train, holding out their hands for sweets.

I had a coupé to myself all the way, and all the time in the world to think of where I was going, what I was leaving behind. And the funny thing was, now that I was going to see the hunter I wasn't at all sure I wanted him. And so, what was the point of the journey? To punish the newspaperman for the things he'd said to me in anger, all of which were true? Truly, it was Leah who was punished, and by mistake too, and when I thought of this, I was sad all over again, marooned in my coupé, moving north through this vast continent because I was wilful and adventurous and I wouldn't give up what I wanted.

And then, at last, I arrived, and there he was, waiting on the platform, which wasn't even a platform, but a mound to step down onto. By now I was mad for him to make sense of the journey for me, to grab me up and tell me things I'd never thought of that way before. But instead he was saying, Did you not receive my telegram? and, Perhaps you aren't aware? And by the time I was loaded with my things into his jalopy, I was full of pity for myself, and close to tears too, which was a thing I knew he hated in a woman.

There were to be two nights and a day together, said he as we bumped along, and then he'd have to be off for a fortnight, and no, he couldn't take me with him, what was I thinking? I'd have to stay in the house with the servants, but it was no place for a white woman and no place for a holiday either.

I just sat beside him, hanging on to the strap with both hands, because the road wasn't a road at all, just tracks in the dust. And not once had he touched me except to hand me up into the jalopy. And I didn't need his warnings about white women and so forth to know that he didn't want me there at all. I was his girl at the port, two or three times a year. And I felt stupid now for the distance I'd traveled, and all the letters I'd sent, the things I'd thought he'd want to hear about me.

Are you cross? said he, smiling at last, a hand coming over to take mine. But I didn't like this either, the smile brought on by my setting myself against him. And so I told him this, and loudly, too, and it was then that he laughed, and stopped the jalopy, and pulled me over to him. I didn't pout, that was never my way, but even though it was lovely to have the smell of him again, and the bitter taste of his tobacco, still I was calculating when the next ship would sail south from Beira, thinking I'd plumb for that, it would be a lovely way to go back.

It was sundown when we arrived at his house, with a great hallooing and the natives running out to stare at me. One woman stood apart, with a half-breed child strapped to her back and another standing at her side. He said something to her in her language, and she stepped forward, looking down at the ground. I knew then that the children must be his, and the mother suffering to see me. She was very black and smooth, with gleaming, round, full breasts and a beaded cloth tied around her hips. And the thought of them together filled me with longing.

He must have known this, because he took me inside, had everything off me at once, even the pins out of my hair. It was dark in the house, hardly a house at all really, just two rooms and a roof made with mud and wooden poles and thatching. It smelled of earth and animal skins and the primus and his tobacco. He hooked up the cloths that closed off the bedroom from the verandah, letting in the last of the afternoon light.

Come, said he, leading me naked out onto the verandah and pointing to a watering hole down the hill, the animals coming in to drink, this kind and that kind, which I pretended to see, but all I could think of was him behind me, breathing on my hair, the salt of his arm when I licked it, and how two things could be felt at once, one for this night and the next, and the other for my future without him in it.

The first thing I did when he left was to make friends with his children. The boy was sober, hiding behind the mother, but the baby was chubby and smiling, and at last, when I gave the mother a comb, she smiled too. The next day, they all came clucking around me, mother and children, holding out their hands like beggars. So I gave them little things, a hair clip, a ribbon, until it got too much altogether, they were shouting and grabbing, and I said, No more, that's enough now. And the mother herself shooed them away.

Every morning she came in at dawn to boil water for the tea. I watched her as she swept the verandah, the beautiful cropped head, and the flat little ears, and then the haunches brilliant in the sun as she squatted at the wheelbarrow to do the washing. And soon it was with his eyes that I was watching her, and the more I watched, the more I wanted her, not for myself but for him, and him for me, and I knew I'd never want him as much any other way.

I brought more things out of my luggage for her. A glass necklace, a brown leather belt. But when she reached out to take them, I held them back, wanting to put them on her myself. We stood face to face as I fastened the necklace, and then buckled the belt around her waist. The skin was firm and strong like rubber, and there was even pleasure in the bitter native smell I'd always found so revolting.

She stared down at the belt with a smile. It looked wonderful on the brown skin, having no purpose there but to decorate it. And then, the next morning, she came wearing a little beaded purse around her neck, and for a moment I thought he must have told her. And so I unbuttoned my bed jacket and showed her mine, and she covered her mouth at the sight, smiling. I took a coin out and called her over and dropped it into her purse. And I didn't put the bed jacket back on again, but lay there with my breasts loose and free like hers. And every night after that I lay naked under the mosquito netting, thinking of her lying there in my place.

And perhaps she thought of me there, too, because one day she came in with a little gift of her own. It was a purse just like hers, which I put on immediately. And, somehow, giving me that gift and seeing it every day around my neck made her less shy. I could get her to join me for tea, although she would drink out of nothing but her own tin mug and sit nowhere but on the floor. When she took a biscuit, she nibbled around the edges like a mouse, and then fed the cream filling to the baby strapped onto her back.

During the heat of the day, we sat in the shade of the verandah, with me reading my old letters. I had found them in a small trunk next to the desk, neatly wrapped in oilcloth. And once again it was as if I were he reading them and also myself writing them, and now here I was, gazing out over the hills, with his woman and her child at my feet. And how could I have thought this up, dreaming as a girl next to the old aga at The Grange, when I was supposed to be peeling potatoes?

And when I'd read the letters and read them through again, then I wrote some new ones. First I wrote to Constance, telling her at last about the hunter, how I'd found him on the *Empress of India* all those years before. And if I'd lied to her then, and for all the years after, well it was because I didn't know how to tell her the truth. The hunter hadn't ever come up between us, and now she was a contented wife and the mother of two children, and who was I to interfere with that?

And then I wrote to Leah. I had never written her a letter before, and couldn't find a way to go about it without sounding nothing like myself. And so I crumpled page after page and threw them to the ground. And there the older boy picked them up and smoothed them out and laid them one on top of the other. So I wrote her about the boy, and how he had only ever used a stick to draw in the sand, and I'd given him a pencil and shown him how to hold it. And now he was drawing an ox or a cow, and I'd include it with my letter. And when I said that I missed her and thought of her every day, I wondered whether she'd know that I was lying. Because, now that I was here, I hardly gave her a thought. It was easy to remember the misery in the taxi and in the train, but I saw that that was a lie as well. It was myself I'd been miserable for, not her, the way life had got hold of my ankle and wouldn't let go. And if I was happy to be there without her, well it was because I felt free again.

And perhaps that was what there had been with the hunter right from the beginning, the two of us down there in the cabin and along the docks, free. And now here I was, and he was everywhere around me more powerfully than if he stood before me. Even the smell and the taste of him were not as true as this.

And then, one day, he stalked up out of the bush with his gun and his bearer in the middle of the afternoon, and never a smile when we first met after an absence, but I could see anyway that he was glad to find me there on his verandah, with my hair hanging free, my legs browned from the sun and bare, and his child playing with the hair-brush at my feet.

Lynn Freed was born and grew up in Durban, South Africa, where two of her previous novels—*Home Ground* and *The Bungalow*—are set. Ms. Freed's stories and essays have appeared in *The New Yorker*, *Harper's*, *Story*, *The New York Times*, *The Washington Post*, and elsewhere. She lives in Sonoma, California.

CHILDREN OF GOD

Mary Doria Russell

Dear BRC Reader,

Mary Russell's debut novel, *The Sparrow,* took us on a journey to a distant planet and into the center of the human soul. It introduced Father Emilio Sandoz, the only member of that original mission to the planet Rakhat to return to Earth. In *Children of God* Father Emilio Sandoz has barely begun to recover from his ordeal when the Society of Jesus calls upon him for help in preparing for another mission. Despite his objections and fear, he cannot escape his past or the future.

Strikingly original, richly plotted, replete with memorable characters and filled with humanity and humor, *Children of God* is an unforgettable and uplifting novel that is a potent successor to *The Sparrow.*

Leona Nevler
Senior Vice-President
and Editorial Director

Naples

September 2060

Sometimes if he kept still, people would go away.

A lay chauffeur had lived here once. The room over the garage was only a few hundred meters from the retreat house, but that was distance enough most of the time, and Emilio Sandoz claimed it for his own with a fierce possessiveness that surprised him. He had added very little to the apartment—photonics, sound equipment, a desk—but it was his. Exposed rafters and plain white walls. Two chairs, a table, a narrow bed; a little kitchen; a shower stall and toilet behind a folding screen.

He accepted that there were things he could not control. The nightmares. The devastating spells of neuralgia, the damaged nerves of his hands sending strobelike bolts of pain up his arms. He'd stopped fighting the crying jags that came without warning; Ed Behr was right, it only made the headaches worse. Here, alone, he could try to roll with the punches—absorb the blows as they came, rest when things eased up. If everyone would just leave him alone—let him handle things at his own pace on his own terms—he'd be all right.

Eyes closed, hunched and rocking over his hands, he waited, straining to hear footsteps retreat from his door. The knocking came again. "Emilio!" It was the Father General's voice and there was a smile in it. "We have an unexpected visitor. Someone has come to meet you."

"Oh, Christ," Sandoz whispered, getting to his feet and tucking his hands under his armpits. He went down the creaking stairs to the side door below and stopped to gather himself, pulling in a ragged breath and letting it out slowly. With a short, sharp movement of his elbow, he flipped the hook out of its eye on the door frame. Waited, doubled over and silent. "All right," he said finally. "It's open."

There was a tall priest standing in the driveway with Giuliani. East African, Sandoz thought, barely glancing at him, his flat-eyed stare resting instead on the Father General's face. "It's not a good time, Vince."

"No," Giuliani said quietly, "evidently not." Emilio was leaning against the wall, holding himself badly, but what could one do? If Lopore had called ahead. . . . "I'm sorry, Emilio. A few minutes of your time. Allow me to—"

"You speak Swahili?" Sandoz asked the visitor abruptly, in a Sudanese-accented Arabic that came back to him out of nowhere. The question seemed to surprise the African, but he nodded. "What else?" Sandoz demanded. "Latin? English?"

"Both of those. A few others," the man said.

"Fine. Good enough. He'll do," Sandoz said to Giuliani. "You'll have to work by yourself for a while," he told the African. "Start with the Mendes AI program for Ruanja. Leave the K'San files alone for now. I didn't get very far with the formal analysis. Next time, call before you come." He glanced at Giuliani, who was clearly dismayed by the rudeness. "Explain about my hands, Vince," he muttered apologetically, as he started back up to his room. "It's both of them. I can't think." And it's your own damned fault for dropping in uninvited, he thought. But he was too close to tears to be defiant, and almost too tired to register what he heard next.

"I have been praying for you for fifty years," said Kalingemala Lopore in a voice full of wonder. "God has used you hard, but you have not changed so much that I cannot see who you were."

Sandoz stopped in his climb to the apartment and turned back. He remained hunched, arms crossed against his chest, but now looked closely at the priest standing next to the Father General. Sixtyish— maybe twenty years younger than Giuliani, and just as tall. Ebony and lean, with the strong bones and deep wide eyes that gave East

African women beauty into old age and which made this man's face arresting. Fifty years, he thought. This guy would have been what? Ten, eleven?

Emilio glanced at Giuliani to see if he understood what was going on, but the Father General now seemed as much at a loss as Sandoz, and as startled by the visitor's words. "Did I know you?" Emilio asked.

The African seemed lit from within, the extraordinary eyes glowing. "There is no reason for you to remember me and I never knew your name. But you were known to God when you were still in your mother's womb—like Jeremiah, whom God also used cruelly." And he held out both hands.

Emilio hesitated before descending the stairs once more. In a gesture that felt, achingly, both familiar and alien, he placed his own fingers, scarred and impossibly long, into the pale, warm palms of the stranger.

All these years, Lopore was thinking, his own shock so great that he forgot the artificiality of the plurals he had forced himself to master. "I remember the magic tricks," he said, smiling, but then he looked down. "Such beauty and cleverness, destroyed," he said sadly and, bringing the hands to his lips, kissed one and then the other unselfconsciously. It was, Sandoz thought later, an alteration in blood pressure perhaps, some quirk of neuromuscular interaction that ended the bout of hallucinatory neuralgia at last, but the African looked up at that moment, and met Emilio's bewildered eyes. "The hands were the easy part, I think."

Sandoz nodded, mute, and frowning, searched the other man's face for some clue.

"Emilio," Vincenzo Giuliani said, breaking the eerie silence, "perhaps you will invite the Holy Father to come upstairs?"

For a hushed instant, Sandoz stared in blank astonishment and then blurted, "Jesus!" To which the Bishop of Rome replied, with unexpected humor, "No, only the Pope," at which the Father General laughed aloud, explaining dryly, "Father Sandoz has been a little out of touch the past few decades."

Dazed, Emilio nodded again and led the way up the staircase.

To be fair, the Pope had come alone and unannounced, dressed in the simplest of clericals, having driven himself in an unremarkable Fiat to the Jesuit retreat north of Naples. The first African elected to the papacy since the fifth century and the first proselyte in modern history to hold that office, Kalingemala Lopore was now Gelasius III, entering the second year of a remarkable reign; he had brought to Rome both a convert's deeply felt conviction and a farsighted faith in the Church's universality, which did not confuse enduring truth with ingrained European custom. At dawn, ignoring politics and diplomatic rigidity, Lopore had decided he must meet this Emilio Sandoz, who had known God's other children, who had seen what God had wrought elsewhere. Having made that decision, there was no bureaucratic force in the Vatican capable of stopping him: Gelasius III was a man of formidable self-possession and unapologetic pragmatism. He was the only outsider ever to get past Sandoz's Camorra guards, and he had done so because he was willing to speak directly with the Father General's second cousin, Don Domenico Giuliani, the uncrowned king of southern Italy.

Sandoz's apartment was a mess, Lopore noted happily as he picked a discarded towel off the nearest chair and tossed it onto the unmade bed, and then sat without ceremony.

"I—I'm sorry about all this," Sandoz stammered, but the Pontiff waved his apology off.

"One of the reasons We insisted on having Our own car was the desire to visit people without setting off an explosion of maniacal preparation," Gelasius III remarked. Then he confided with specious formality, "We find We are thoroughly sick of fresh paint and new carpeting." He motioned for Emilio to take the other seat, across the table from him. "Please," he said, dropping the plurals deliberately, "sit with me." But he glanced at Giuliani, standing in the corner near the stairway, unwilling to intrude but loath to leave. Stay, the Holy Father's eyes said, and remember everything.

"My people are Dodoth. Herders, even now," the Pope told Sandoz, his Latin exotic with African place names and the rhythmic, striding cadences of his childhood. "When the drought came, we went north to our cousins, the Toposa, in southern Sudan. It was a time of war and so, of famine. The Toposa drove us off—they had nothing. We asked, 'Where can we go?' A man on the road told us, 'There is a camp for Gikuyu east of here. They turn no one away.' It was a long journey and, as we walked, my youngest sister died in my mother's arms. You saw us coming. You walked out to my family. You took from my mother her daughter's body, as gently as if the baby were your own. You carried that dead child and found us a place to rest. You brought us water, and then food. While we ate, you dug a grave for my sister. Do you recall now?"

"No. There were so many babies. So many dead." Emilio looked up wearily. "I have dug a lot of graves, Your Holiness."

"There will be no more graves for you to dig," the Pope said, and Vincenzo Giuliani heard the voice of prophesy: ambiguous, elusive, sure. The moment passed and the Pontiff's conversation became ordinary again. "Every day of my life since that one, I have thought of you! What kind of man weeps for a daughter not of his making? The answer to that question led me to Christianity, to the priesthood, and now: here, to you!" He sat back in the chair, amazed that he should meet that unknown priest half a century later. He paused and then continued gently, a priest himself, whose office was to reconcile God and man. "You have wept for other children since those days in the Sudan."

"Hundreds. More. Thousands, I think, died because of me."

"You take a great deal on your shoulders. But there was one child in particular, We are told. Can you speak her name, so that We may remember her in prayer?"

He could, but only barely, almost without sound. "Askama, Your Holiness."

There was silence for a time and then Kalingemala Lopore reached across the small table, lifting Emilio's bowed head with blunt, strong fingers, and smoothing away the tears. Vincenzo Giuliani had always thought of Emilio as dark, but with those powerful brown hands cupping his face, he looked ghostly, and then Giuliani realized that Sandoz had nearly fainted. Emilio hated being touched, loathed unexpected contact. Lopore could not have known this and Giuliani took a step forward, about to explain, when he realized that the Pope was speaking.

Emilio listened, stone-faced, with the quick shallow movement of the chest that sometimes betrayed him. Giuliani could not hear their words, but he saw Sandoz freeze, and pull away, and stand and begin to pace. "I made a cloister of my body and a garden of my soul, Your Holiness. The stones of the cloister wall were my nights, and my days were the mortar," Emilio said in the soft, musical Latin that a young Vince Giuliani had admired and envied when they were in formation together. "Year after year, I built the walls. But in the center I made a garden that I left open to heaven, and I invited God to walk there. And God came to me." Sandoz turned away, trembling. "God filled me, and the rapture of those moments was so pure and so powerful that the cloister walls were leveled. I had no more need for walls, Your Holiness. God was my protection. I could look into the face of the wife I would never have, and love all wives. I could look into the face of the husband I would never be, and love all husbands. I could dance at weddings because I was in love with God, and all the children were mine."

Giuliani, stunned, felt his eyes fill. Yes, he thought. Yes.

But when Emilio turned again and faced Kalingemala Lopore, he was not weeping. He came back to the table and placed his ruined hands on its battered wood, face rigid with rage. "And now the garden is laid waste," he whispered. "The wives and the husbands and the children are all dead. And there is nothing left but ash and bone. Where was our Protector? Where was God, Your Holiness? Where is God now?"

The answer was immediate, certain. "In the ashes. In the bones. In the souls of the dead, and in the children who live because of you—"

"Nothing lives because of me!"

"You're wrong. I live. And there are others."

"I am a blight. I carried death to Rakhat like syphilis, and God laughed while I was raped."

"God wept for you. You have paid a terrible price for His plan, and God wept when He asked it of you—"

Sandoz cried out and backed away, shaking his head. "That is the most terrible lie of all! God does not ask. I gave no consent. The dead gave no consent. God is not innocent."

The blasphemy hung in the room like smoke, but it was joined seconds later by Jeremiah's. "He hath led me and brought me into darkness, and not into light. He hath set me in dark places as those who are dead forever. And when I cry and I entreat," Gelasius III recited, eyes knowing and full of compassion, "He hath shut out my prayer! He hath filled me with bitterness. He hath fed me ashes. He hath caused me disgrace and contempt."

Sandoz stood still and stared at nothing they could see. "I am damned," he said finally, tired to his soul, "and I don't know why."

Kalingemala Lopore sat back in his chair, the long, strong fingers folded loosely in his lap, his faith in hidden meaning, and in God's work in God's time, granitic. "You are beloved of God," he said. "And you will live to see what you have made possible when you return to Rakhat."

Sandoz's head snapped up. "I won't go back."

"And if you are asked to do so by your superior?" Lopore asked, brows up, glancing at Giuliani.

Vincenzo Giuliani, forgotten until now in his corner, found himself looking into Emilio Sandoz's eyes and was, for the first time in some fifty-five years, utterly cowed. He spread his hands and shook his head, beseeching Emilio to believe: I didn't put him up to this.

"*Non serviam,*" Sandoz said, turning from Giuliani. "I won't be used again."

"Not even if We ask it?" the Pope pressed.

"No."

"So. Not for the Society. Not for Holy Mother Church. Nevertheless, for yourself and for God, you must go back," Gelasius III told Emilio Sandoz with a terrifying, joyful certainty. "God is waiting for you, in the ruins."

Mary Doria Russell lives in Cleveland, Ohio, ("and likes it very much, thank you") with her husband, Don, and their son, Daniel. She is currently working on a historical thriller about the Jewish underground in Genoa during the Nazi occupation of Italy. "There are extraordinary stories of rescue and resistance in northern Italy," says Russell, "and they deserve to be better known. We've spent fifty years trying to understand what went wrong in most of Europe—it's time to look at what went right in Italy, where 80 percent of Italian Jews survived the occupation, and where thousands of European refugees found welcome and shelter and support."

SAINTS AND VILLAINS

Denise Giardina

Dear BRC Reader,

Saints and Villains is a big dramatic novel which is also a triumphant portrayal of one of the authentic heroes of the twentieth century, as well as a profound drama of the meaning of faith, morality, and love of country played out amid the rise and fall of the Third Reich. It is about a real historical figure, Dietrich Bonhoeffer, the German theologian and Nazi resister who risked his life smuggling Jews out of Germany and ultimately lost it through his participation in the failed plot to assassinate Hitler.

Leona Nevler
Senior Vice-President
and Editorial Director

He longed to be a scholar hidden away in a dormered attic room lined on all sides with books, so that no matter which way he swiveled in his chair—and of course the chair must swivel—he would see thick volumes of theology. He wanted to emerge from this room groggy from his studies and wander to Berlin University, where he would deliver lectures of such density his students would not be able to look up from their note-taking. They would whisper about him afterward, shake their heads and wonder what sort of life he must lead. He would enjoy the speculation. He wanted to be wildly, luxuriously eccentric, instead of what he was becoming—practical, organized, and a writer only of pamphlets.

He began to think of the students as his enemies. When he posted notices of meetings on the Christian response to the new government, they were ripped down. More and more university scholars sported shiny gold-and-enamel swastika pins on their lapels. They stood in the middle of Dietrich's lectures with a great show of slamming notebooks, and walked out. He tried to ignore the interruptions, though his face reddened as he bent over his notes and sought to control his voice. But the most disconcerting challenge came in the customary way. A young man with the face of an angel and bearing on that face the look of aggrieved youth smitten with divine knowledge raised his hand at the end of a lecture.

Dietrich paused as he straightened his notes. "Yes, Herr ah—?"

"Bielenberg."

"Herr Bielenberg. Your question?"

"In fact, a complaint, Herr Professor."

Dietrich noted the swastika pin on Bielenberg's lapel and held his breath.

"You speak of theology as an intellectual pursuit, Herr Professor, which implies openness to ideas. Yet you consistently trample upon the sensibilities of your students."

"In what way?"

"You have no respect for our opinions. And no openness toward the new thinking in Germany."

"Hear, hear," someone called from the back of the lecture hall.

"You wish to force everyone to think as you do," said Bielenberg. "You are narrow-minded. In addition you are unnecessarily negative when you speak of the Fatherland. We students want open-mindedness, not a simplistic parroting of liberal nonsense. Is that too much to expect from the lecturers of this university?"

These remarks were greeted by thunderous applause. Dietrich searched for a response, but his mind seemed to have turned to glue. He, narrow-minded? An enforcer of prescribed opinion because he appealed to reason and tolerance and Christian charity? As he groped for an answer the students were leaving the lecture hall, filing out with loud guffaws and much back-slapping, or moving in small packs toward Bielenberg to pump his hand.

Dietrich navigated the marble staircase to Unter den Linden and crossed to the garden beside the State Opera House. There he slumped on a stone bench in the growing darkness, gulping the winter air like a thirsty man at a cold stream, and knew he would not stay much longer at the university.

Although his pamphlets were not at all what he would have liked to spend his time writing, he tried to think of them as theology of a practical sort. This was something of a comfort. He neglected his other work, for always he was attending meetings, organizing meetings, speaking at meetings, in an effort to prod the Church into some response. Day after day he sat in drab parish halls, dragging on one cigarette after another and blowing smoke toward ceilings mottled with brown watermarks while this one fretted, "Hitler may be a bit hard on the Jews," and that one responded, "Of course he's only huffing and puffing, it plays well to the crowd and makes for a color-ful speech," and another said, "Doesn't hurt to have a bit of a shaking all round, wake everyone up."

Sometimes resolutions were passed. Most of the time nothing was done and more meetings were called.

One saving grace was that Elisabeth often accompanied him. He enjoyed her company most when they traveled together, driving from town to town in Brandenburg and Saxony and Thuringia with bundles of pamphlets stuffed in the boot of the family Mercedes. At the end of a meeting they escaped whatever stuffy parish hall they'd been in and headed to a café for strudel dredged with cream, and cof-fee. As though the Political Situation, as they called it, had taken on the role of organizer of their social calendar. Dietrich liked to be seen with her, especially when she laughed at him, covering her mouth with one hand and opening her eyes wide, or leaned back in her chair so that her short dark hair fell away from her face. They held hands beneath the table. He imagined other men might be envious, that el-derly women sitting across the room watched them with pleasure and recalled their own first love.

Their time alone was different. Dietrich enjoyed holding her close, liked to kiss her and run his fingers through her hair, around her neck, and down the curve of her back before undressing her and tak-ing her into his bed. But when all was done he felt a nagging empti-ness in the pit of his stomach, even as he held her close. For he wasn't certain he loved her enough to marry her, and in such circumstances he thought it wrong, very wrong, to be sleeping with her.

He admitted this to himself at Friedrichsbrunn, though he hadn't the courage to tell Elisabeth then. The drive to the Harz Mountains with the wounded Falk Harnack, hidden beneath a bearskin rug so not even the top of his head showed, had been quiet and tense. Ex-hausted even before setting out, they were forced to take turns rest-ing and driving, so that whoever was awake had no company but the sounds of the road and the sleep-heavy breathing of the other. Dawn broke well before they arrived. Outside Quedlinburg they ran low on petrol, but Dietrich was afraid to pull up to a pump. Instead he stopped a quarter of a mile past a station and hiked back, purchased petrol in a can, and returned to the Mercedes.

Friedrichsbrunn was not what Elisabeth had expected. When Die-trich had talked of the Bonhoeffer vacation home in the Harz Moun-tains, she had imagined a half-timbered lodge nestled in an isolated hollow. But the Friedrichsbrunn house was ugly, a squat structure of brick studded with gables, one of several houses in an open field between the village and the woods. Dietrich drove the Mercedes across the frozen garden and pulled up beside the back door. Falk was awake and summoned enough strength to stumble into the house supported on either side by Dietrich and Elisabeth. It was broad daylight, impossible to hide their arrival, but no one in the village seemed about, and no one stopped by, even after Dietrich built a fire in the bedroom grate.

"They'll notice the smoke," Elisabeth said, "and know someone's here."

"Yes," said Dietrich. "But to be honest, we keep mostly to ourselves here, and people in the village have never paid much attention to us. Except for the families who run the guesthouses, they're rather insular."

As are you Bonhoeffers, Elisabeth thought. She went downstairs to search for food. In the cellar she found a bin of potatoes and onions, butts of crusty ham and salt beef suspended from rafters, and a rack of dusty wine bottles. The pantry held a round white cheese, tins of herring, and bottles of brandy and schnapps. Back upstairs, where Dietrich had changed Falk's dressing and put him to bed, she said, "I was afraid there'd be no food. But it looks as though we could survive here all winter."

Falk, groggy again, mumbled, "Something hot to drink?"

Elisabeth patted his blanket. "You'll have a toddy very soon, and something to eat. And your brother will come as well." She looked at Dietrich. "Won't he?"

"I hope. If Suse has got hold of him."

Arvid Harnack arrived sooner than expected. Suse had quickly reached him, and he had driven through the night with his American wife, Mildred. Mildred possessed the blunt optimism and aura of self-sufficiency Dietrich had noted before—and been disconcerted by—in American women. When she saw the haggard-looking Falk, she said quite cheerfully, "Oh dear, our boy will need some rest, won't he."

Falk blinked up at her. "Mildred," he croaked, "where will you take me?"

She sat on the edge of the bed and patted his hand. "You'll come home with us to Munich, of course. We'll fatten you up, and then you can get back to your work in the theater. How does that sound?"

He nodded and shut his eyes. "It's not so bad then?"

Arvid, a taller, thinner, and bespectacled version of Falk, said, "It's still Germany, of course, no matter who's chancellor."

"Of course," Mildred said briskly. "All this will blow over soon enough. The German people won't be ruled by such idiots."

They ate sandwiches, huddled around the hearth in Falk's room for warmth, then carried Falk to the Harnacks' waiting car. Arvid and Dietrich shook hands, Mildred kissed Elisabeth on the cheek, and the Harnacks were gone. Dietrich and Elisabeth stood arm in arm in front of the house.

"Are Americans always so cheerful?" she asked.

Dietrich laughed. "They're in love with happy endings. And the women can be a bit pushy."

"Oh?" Elisabeth looked up at him. "I didn't think so. I quite liked her, actually."

They walked through the garden to the back of the house. A clear midwinter sun lit the pasture with a brown glow, and the dark looming woods were shot through at the edges with threads of light. In the distance the carpet of forest ran up the haphazard folds of the Harz.

"I'm beginning to understand the attraction of Friedrichsbrunn," Elisabeth said.

"They're wonderful woods to walk in," said Dietrich. "All rises and ravines. One expects at any moment to encounter a goblin or a Walpurgis Night witch."

"Are there lonely cottages?"

"Oh, yes, and abandoned pilgrims' crosses and bears who once were princes. Shall we stay a day or two? Or do you want to go back to Berlin tonight?"

"I'm so tired," Elisabeth said. "Let's stay."

Dietrich had daydreamed of bringing a new wife to Friedrichsbrunn on honeymoon. Most women he knew (of the few women he knew) would have wanted to go to Paris or Rome. But Elisabeth was the Friedrichsbrunn type. She liked the outdoors and had a vigorous way of walking, head up and footsteps loud as she plowed along paths crusty with old snow. The cold air quickened her face behind the white veil of her own frozen breath. Elisabeth should fit very well in the Friedrichsbrunn daydream.

Except Dietrich was not happy. He put it down to guilt. He was deeply old-fashioned where marriage was concerned. The teachings of the Roman church on divorce seemed admirable to him, much to the dismay and amusement of his brothers and sisters. Marriage was a sacrament, he argued, a sign of grace, and once undertaken with vows to one's partner and to God, it must last forever. How then, Suse once asked, would anyone dare to marry? Perhaps, he'd answered, few *should* marry. And he'd thought what a frightening responsibility it was, to commit to a single person for the rest of one's life. Suppose one's chosen mate failed in some terribly important way? Suppose she, for example, proved shallow, had only pretended to love Bach so as to impress the other, or read only trivial romantic fiction, or became a hypochondriac, or secretly admired Hitler? Or, or, or? There were a thousand ways to disappoint Dietrich.

And if marriage was sacred, how dare he sleep with his future wife without the benefit of the sacrament, especially at Friedrichsbrunn, his family's home?

When they came in from their late walk in the Friedrichsbrunn woods, he said, "Since we're both so tired, perhaps we should sleep in separate rooms. It would be more restful."

She looked surprised. "Why? Is something wrong?"

"No. Of course not."

She would not be put off. "What is it? One of your depressions? If you're wanting time alone I can entertain myself. But we'd be warmer sleeping together. You'd have to build another fire otherwise, and we may not have enough wood."

He was suddenly angry that she would reduce the situation to a practical level, and saying nothing, went across the hall to the doorway of the room he slept in when the family was in residence. It was a long, narrow alcove that lay in shadow, and the windows were laced with hard frost.

She came to stand behind him. "It looks as though it misses the sun," she said.

He reluctantly admitted that the room was one of the coolest in the house because it sheltered beneath the close-standing oak and lacked direct sun, making it much prized in the summer months. And as he spoke she reached beneath his jacket and ran her hand up his spine and let it rest beneath his shoulder blades. He pulled her close and rested his cheek on the top of her head, knew he would give in to desire once again.

* * *

Back in Berlin they visited the service at Elisabeth's home parish of Annenkirche in Dahlem. They sat in the last pew. During the lessons, Dietrich's attention wandered. He studied the walls, tried to imagine the former glory of the faded medieval paintings which hovered ghostlike just beneath the thin surface of whitewash. Elisabeth interrupted his reverie to point out this or that distinguished parishioner. "General von Hammerstein-Equord," she said in his ear. "Friedrich Dietlof Graf von der Schulenburg. Major Hans Oster."

Dietrich studied Hans Oster with mild interest, because he had heard Hans von Dohnanyi mention him recently. Oster, Dohnanyi thought, might be One of Us. But Oster was also in disgrace for conducting an affair with the wife of a senior officer. He sat now beside his own wife (no farther away from her than Dietrich sat from Elisabeth), eyes on the pulpit, with an iron-straight posture that can only be achieved by a military man or a fanatic.

Pastor Martin Niemöller was preaching. His sermon, which Dietrich carefully evaluated, was noncommittal (taking its text, as required, from one of the many verses in the Gospel of John which meditated on Jesus as the bread of life). The ending was more to the point—there is only one God, and He is already known to us. After the service, as Niemöller shook the hands of departing parishioners, he grabbed Dietrich by the arm—"Ah, yes, Pastor Bonhoeffer, I know why you are here"—and motioned him aside. Dietrich and Elisabeth waited outside, at the edge of the crowded cemetery with its maze of snow-capped headstones and shrubbery. When the crowd had cleared, Niemöller, a thin man with a wizened face that made him look older than his years, came to them and said, "I would take you home with me"—a large comfortable-looking brick house with a bay window that overlooked the church—"but my wife has influenza and I don't like to disturb the quiet. However, the Café Luise is just down the street."

So they ended in the front room of the Luise, overlooking the frozen beer garden, which in summer would be filled with shirtsleeved men and women in cotton frocks talking over round iron tables. They ate plates of schnitzel and buttery noodles washed down with red wine.

"Now," Niemöller said, chewing his words as vigorously as his meat, "we must deal with this Hitler fellow. He must be made to understand he can't dictate to the church as he does to those brownshirts of his."

Dietrich nodded.

"On the other hand," Niemöller continued, "I look for some good in him. Do you know what I hear from my parishioners?—and many of them are highly placed in government, as I'm sure you know. Hitler will soon take us out of the League of Nations." He hefted the bottle of burgundy. "More wine?" And smiled. "That will be something, anyway."

Elisabeth drove back to the Grunewald while Dietrich stared moodily out the window.

"He was a hero in the Great War," Elisabeth pointed out. "A U-boat commander. Not that that excuses him. But you have complained about the Versailles Treaty yourself."

"When was the last time you attended one of his services?" Dietrich asked abruptly.

"It's been a while," she said. "Over a year. We've been all over the place on weekends, you and I—"

"That's not the only reason," he said.

"No," she said, "not the only reason. I'm not comfortable in church. I only go with you for the company, and because I believe in our work. But I'm not so sure, Dietrich, what I believe anymore. Or who I am."

"Who you are?"

She drove for a time, careful to avoid the rims of hard snow on the shoulders of the roadway.

"Every day," she said, "I feel more like a Jew. I'm not sure about the rest."

That night they went to bed in her apartment and lay without touching, their faces turned toward the window, watching clumps of snow flutter against the pane.

At last she said, "We don't have to go on, you know. Not if you don't want to."

" You're moving away from me," he said. "You're becoming a different person."

She sat up and pulled the quilt tight around her. "Don't dare blame me."

"I don't mean—" he stammered, trying to think how to continue. "Elisabeth, I do care about you."

"I know you care about me," she said. "I'm not sure how much."

"You know how I feel about marriage."

"God knows we've argued enough about that," she said. "You're the most old-fashioned man I know."

He raised up on one elbow and said almost eagerly, "Then doesn't it seem strange for me to be here in bed with you?"

She shut her eyes.

"That first night—" he searched for words "—it was as though the world had turned upside down. As though normal ways of behaving had gone out the window. At least normal for me. But I'm getting my bearings again."

He waited for her to answer. When she was silent he continued, "I can't sleep with you again. At least, not until we're married. And I'm not ready to marry."

She turned her face away and nodded.

"I'm sorry," he said.

She put her hand to her face and sobbed. He stroked her arm, feeling miserable, and said, "I still want to see you. I want everything else to be exactly the same. Except, a step back please, from this. At least, for now. And I need your help because God knows I find you attractive and it is easy for me to give in to that. So I must ask you not to initiate any physical—"

"Then you should go," she managed to say.

He dressed quickly, after stepping away from the snow-lit window into shadow, as though modesty would erase past intimacy.

When he went to the door she said, "We may not be able to go on as before. Men who feel bad usually blame the woman."

"I won't," he said. He came back then and sat on the edge of the bed, pushed the hair from her forehead with one large hand. "There is no blame, only gratitude." He bent and kissed her forehead. "And there is a future. I just need some time."

She touched his cheek and shook her head. "We'll see," she said. And used the rest of her tears when he had gone.

In his room high up in Wangenheimstraße 14, in the privileged quiet of the Grunewald, Dietrich listens to the radio. It is not what he should be doing. He should be writing. Instead he sits at his desk, sips a glass of wine.

He turns the dial ever so slowly. The radio crackles and squawks—

interrupted now and then by a low, soothing voice, a wisp of violin music or quiet French horn—

Except for the clearest frequency, the RRG, which erupts with Adolf Hitler in full cry, answered by the clamor of a cheering throng—a broadcast from the Sportpalast. It is the first political rally to be carried live on radio.

Dietrich listens, chin resting in hand. He is alone and yet he is not, for the Nazis have provided radio receivers at nominal cost to anyone who can scrape together a few marks. This is the idea of Goebbels, who dreams of millions of Germans, even the poorest Germans, sitting with hands on chins before their new receivers. Next Goebbels will imagine everyone listening to the same thing.

Unlike Dietrich, who quickly tires of Hitler's tirade despite a desire to learn more about what the Nazis are up to. He shakes his head and decides this new tactic will fail, for how will anyone be able to bear the stale jokes and forced humor, the historical inaccuracies, spiritual vapidity, and upside-down logic that characterize Hitler's speech?

He concentrates again on the dial and at last picks up a distant thump and wail. He turns up the volume. Swing music from the BBC. Chick Webb and his orchestra.

Dietrich shuts his eyes tight, and the wine and the music bring him to tears.

DENISE GIARDINA, the author of three previous novels, teaches at West Virginia State College in Charleston, West Virginia. She is a licensed lay preacher in the Episcopal Church.

A PATCHWORK PLANET

Anne Tyler

Dear BRC Reader,

The essence of Anne Tyler's great art is that she writes about ordinary people in an extraordinary way. She writes with compassion and tenderness about their missteps and misfortunes without ever losing sight of the comedy in their lives.

A Patchwork Planet is the story of Barnaby Gaitlin, a lovable loser. Not quite thirty, already divorced, he is trying to live down his teenage irresponsibility and get his disorderly life in order. The black sheep of an affluent Baltimore family, Barnaby works steadily for Rent-a-Back, renting his efforts and winning the adoration of old folks and shut-ins who can't do their own chores, but neither his parents nor his ex-wife trust him. When he meets Sophia, sensible, steady, principled, he thinks he may have finally found the guardian who can straighten out the rest of his life.

Leona Nevler
Senior Vice-President
and Editorial Director

I am a man you can trust, is how my customers view me. Or at least, I'm guessing it is. Why else would they hand me their house keys before they leave for vacation? Why else would they depend on me to clear their attics for them, heave their air conditioners into their windows every spring, lug their excess furniture to their basements? "Mind your step, young fellow; that's Hepplewhite," Mrs. Rodney says, and then she goes into her kitchen to brew a pot of tea. I could get up to anything in that basement. I could unlock the outside door so as to slip back in overnight and rummage through all she owns— her Hepplewhite desk and her Japanese lacquer jewelry box and the six potbellied drawers of her dining-room buffet. Not that I would. But she doesn't know that. She just assumes it. She takes it for granted that I'm a good person.

Come to think of it, I am the one who doesn't take it for granted.

On the very last day of a bad old year, I was leaning against a pillar in the Baltimore railroad station, waiting to catch the 10:10 a.m. to Philadelphia. Philadelphia's where my little girl lives. Her mother married a lawyer there after we split up.

Ordinarily I'd have driven, but my car was in the shop and so I'd had to fork over the money for a train ticket. *Scads* of money. Not to mention being some appointed place at some appointed time, which I hate. Plus, there were a lot more people waiting than I had expected. That airy, light, clean, varnished feeling I generally got in Penn Station had been crowded out. Elderly couples with matching luggage stuffed the benches, and swarms of college kids littered the floor with their duffel bags. This gray-haired guy was walking around speaking to different strangers one by one. Well-off guy, you could tell: tan skin, nice turtleneck, soft beige car coat. He went up to a woman sitting alone and asked her a question. Then he came over to a girl in a miniskirt standing near me. I had been thinking I wouldn't mind talking to her myself. She had long blond hair, longer than her skirt, which made it seem she'd neglected to put on the bottom half of her outfit. The man said, "Would you by any chance be traveling to Philadelphia?"

"Well, northbound, yes," she said, in this shallow, breathless voice that came as a disappointment.

"But to Philadelphia?"

"No, New York, but I'll be—"

"Thanks anyway," he said, and he moved toward the next bench.

Now he had my full attention. "Ma'am," I heard him ask an old lady, "are you traveling to Philadelphia?" The old lady answered something too mumbly for me to catch, and instantly he turned to the woman beside her. "Philadelphia?" Notice how he was getting more and more sparing of words. When the woman told him, "Wilmington," he didn't say a thing; just plunged on down the row to one of the matched-luggage couples. I straightened up from my pillar and drifted closer, looking toward Gate E as if I had my mind on my train. The wife was telling the man about their New Year's plans. They were baby-sitting their grandchildren who lived in New York City, she said, and the husband said, "Well, not New York City proper, dear; White Plains," and the gray-haired man, almost shouting, said, "But my daughter's counting on me!" And off he raced.

Well, *I* was going to Philadelphia. He could have asked me. I understood why he didn't, of course. No doubt I struck him as iffy, with my three-day growth of black stubble and my ripped black leather jacket and my jeans all dust and cobwebs from Mrs. Morey's garage. But still he could have given me a chance. Instead he just flicked his eyes at me and then swerved off toward the bench at the end of the room. By now he was looking seriously undermedicated. "Please!" he said to a woman reading a book. "Tell me you're going to Philadelphia!"

She lowered her book. She was thirtyish, maybe thirty-five—older than I was, anyhow. A schoolmarm sort, in a wide brown coat with a pattern like feathers all over it. "Philadelphia?" she said. "Why, yes, I am."

"Then could I ask you a favor?"

I stopped several feet away and frowned down at my left wrist. (Never mind that I don't own a watch.) Even without looking, I could sense how she went on guard. The man must have sensed it too, because he said, "Nothing too difficult, I promise!"

They were announcing my train now. ("The delayed 10:10," the loudspeaker called it. It's always "the delayed" this or that.) People started moving toward Gate E, the older couples hauling their wheeled bags behind them like big, meek pets on leashes. If the woman in the feather coat said anything, I missed it. Next I heard, the man was talking. "My daughter's flying out this afternoon for a junior semester abroad," he was saying. "Leaving from Philadelphia; the airline offers a bargain rate if you leave from Philadelphia. So I put her on a train this morning, stopped for groceries afterward, and came home to find my wife in a state. It seems our daughter'd forgotten her passport. She'd telephoned from the station in Philly; didn't know what to do next."

The woman clucked sympathetically. I'd have kept quiet myself. Waited to find out where the guy was heading with this.

"So I told her she should stay put. Stay right there in the station, I said, and I would get somebody here to carry up her passport."

A likely story! Why didn't he go himself, if this was such an emergency?

"Why don't you go yourself?" the woman asked him.

"I can't leave my wife alone that long. She's in a wheelchair: Parkinson's."

This seemed like a pretty flimsy excuse, if you want my honest opinion. Also, it exceeded what I would consider the normal quota for misfortunes. Not only a lamebrain daughter, but a wife with a major disease! I let my eyes wander toward the two of them. The woman was gazing up into the man's face, pooching her mouth out thoughtfully. The man was holding a packet. He must have pulled it from his car coat: not a manila envelope, which would have been the logical choice, but one of those padded mailers the size of a paperback book. Aha! Padded! So you couldn't feel the contents! And from where I stood, it looked to be stapled shut besides. *Watch yourself, lady,* I said silently.

As if she'd heard me, she told the man, "I hope this isn't some kind of contraband." Except she pronounced it "counterband," which made me think she must not be a schoolmarm, after all.

"No, no!" the man told her. He gave a huff of a laugh. "No, I can assure you it's not counterband."

Was he repeating her mistake on purpose? I couldn't tell. (Or maybe the word really *was* "counterband.") Meanwhile, the loud-speaker came to life again. The delayed 10:10 was now boarding. Train wheels squealed below me. "I'll do it," the woman decided.

"Oh, wonderful! That's wonderful! Thanks!" the man told her, and he handed her the packet. She was already rising. Instead of a suitcase, she had one of those tote things that could have been just a large purse, and she fitted the strap over her shoulder and lined up the packet with the book she'd been reading. "So let's see," the man was saying. "You've got light-colored hair, you're wearing a brown print coat. . . . I'll call the pay phone where my daughter's waiting and let her know who to watch for. She'll be standing at Information when you get there. Esther Brimm, her name is—a redhead. You can't miss that hair of hers. Wearing jeans and a blue-jean jacket. Ask if she's Esther Brimm."

He followed the woman through the double doors and down the stairs, although he wasn't supposed to. I was close behind. The cold felt good after the packed waiting room. "And you are?" the man was asking.

Affected way of putting it. They arrived on the platform and stopped short, so that I just about ran over them. The woman said, "I'm Sophia—" and then something like "Maiden" that I couldn't ex-actly hear. (The train was in place but rumbling, and passengers were clip-clopping by.) "In case we miss connections, though . . . ," she said, raising her voice.

In case they missed connections, he should put his name and phone number on the mailer. Any fool would know that much. But he seemed to have his mind elsewhere. He said, "Um . . . now, do you live in Baltimore? I mean, are you coming *back* to Baltimore, or is Philly your end destination?"

I almost laughed aloud at that. So! Already he'd forgotten he was grateful; begun to question his angel of mercy's reliability. But she didn't take offense. She said, "Oh, I'm a *long*-time Baltimorean. This is just an overnight visit to my mother. I do it every weekend: take the ten-ten Patriot Saturday morning and come back sometime Sunday."

"Well, then!" he said. "Well. I certainly do appreciate this."

"It's no trouble at all," she said, and she smiled and turned to board.

I had been hoping to sit next to her. I was planning to start a conversation—mention I'd overheard what the man had asked of her and then suggest the two of us check the contents of his packet. But the car was nearly full, and she settled down beside a lady in a fur hat. The closest I could manage was across the aisle to her left and one row back, next to a black kid wearing earphones. Only view I had was a schoolmarm's netted yellow bun and a curve of cheek.

Well, anyhow, why was I making this out to be such a big deal? Just bored, I guess. I shucked my jacket off and sat forward to peer in my seat-back pocket. A wrinkly McDonald's bag, a napkin stained with ketchup, a newspaper section folded to the crossword puzzle. The puzzle was only half done, but I didn't have a pen on me. I looked over at the black kid. He probably didn't have a pen, either, and anyhow he was deep in his music—long brown fingers tapping time on his knees.

Then just beyond him, out the window, I chanced to notice the passport man talking on the phone. Talking on the phone? Down here beside the tracks? Sure enough: one of those little cell phones you all the time see obnoxious businessmen showing off in public. I leaned closer to the window. Something here was weird, I thought. Maybe he smuggled drugs, or worked for the CIA. Maybe he was a terrorist. I wished I knew how to read lips. But already he was closing his phone, slipping it into his pocket, turning to go back upstairs. And our train was sliding out of the station.

I looked again at the woman. At the packet, to be specific.

It was resting on top of her book, which sat in her feather-print lap. (She would be the type who stayed properly buttoned into her coat, however long the trip.) Where the mailer was folded over, staples ran straight across in a nearly unbroken line. But staples were no problem. She could pry them up with, say, a nail file or a dime, and slip them out undetectably, and replace them when she was finished. *Do it,* I told her in my head. She was gazing past her seatmate, out the right-hand window. I couldn't even see her cheek now; just her bun.

Back in the days when I was a juvenile delinquent, I used to break into houses and read people's private mail. Also photo albums. I had a real thing about photo albums. The other kids who broke in along with me, they'd be hunting car keys and cigarettes and booze. They'd be tearing through closets and cabinets all around me, while I sat on the sofa poring over somebody's wedding pictures. And even when I took stuff, it was always personal stuff. This little snow globe once from a nightstand in a girl's bedroom. Another time, a brass egg that stood on scaly claw feet and opened to show a snapshot of an old-fashioned baby inside. I'm not proud of this. I'd sooner confess to jewel theft than to pocketing six letters tied up with satin ribbon, which is what I did when we jimmied the lock at the Empreys' place one night. But there you are. What can I say.

So when this Sophia woman let the packet stay untouched—didn't prod it, didn't shake it, didn't tease apart the merest corner of the flap—I felt something like, oh, almost envy. A huge wave of envy. I started wishing *I* could be like that. Man, I'd have been tearing into that packet with my bare teeth, if I'd had the chance.

The conductor came and went, and the row houses slipping by turned into factory buildings and then to matted woods and a sheet of gray water, but I was barely conscious of anything beyond Sophia's packet. I saw how quietly her hands rested on the brown paper; she was not a fidgeter. Smooth, oval nails, pale pink, and plump white fingers like a woman's in a religious painting. Her book was turned the wrong way for me to read the title, but I knew it was something worthwhile and educational. Oh, these people who prepare ahead! Who think to bring actual books, instead of dashing into a newsstand at the last minute for a *Sports Illustrated* or—worse yet—making do with a crossword puzzle that someone else has started!

It bothered me more than I liked to admit that the passport man had avoided me.

We were getting close to Wilmington, and the lady in the fur hat started collecting her things. After she left, I planned to change seats. I would wait for Sophia to shift over to the window, and then I'd sit down next to her. "Morning," I would say. "Interesting packet you've got there."

"I see you're carrying some kind of packet."

"Mind if I inquire what's in that packet?"

Or whatever. Something would come to me. But when the train stopped and the lady stood up, Sophia just turned her knees to one side to let her out. She stayed seated where she was, on the aisle, so I didn't see any natural-seeming way to make my move.

We left Wilmington behind. We traveled past miles of pipeline and smokestacks, some of them belching flames. I could tell now that it was rap music the kid beside me was listening to. He had the volume raised so high that I could hear it winding out of his earphones—that chanting and insisting sound like the voices you hear in your dreams.

"Philll-adelphia!" the conductor called.

Of course Sophia got ready too soon. We were barely in sight of the skyline—bluish buildings shining in the pale winter sunlight, Liberty Towers scalloping their way up and up and up—but she was already rising to wait in the aisle. The exit lay to the rear, and so she had to face me. I could see the pad of flesh that was developing under her chin. She leaned against her seat and teetered gently with the swaying of the car. *Critics are unanimous!* the back of her book said. The mailer was almost hidden between the book and her cushiony bosom.

I put on my jacket, but I didn't stand up yet. I waited till the train had come to a stop and she had passed me. Then I swung out into the aisle lickety-split, cutting in front of a fat guy with a briefcase. I followed Sophia so closely, I could smell the dusty smell of her coat. It was velvet, or something like velvet. Velvet always smells dusty, even when it's fresh from the cleaners.

There was the usual scuffle with that automatic door that likes to squash the passengers—Press the button, dummies!—and the usual milling and nudging in the vestibule, and then we stepped out into a rush of other people. It was obvious that Sophia knew where she was going. She didn't so much as glance around her but walked fast, coming down hard on her heels. Her heels were the short, chunky kind, but they made her as tall as I was. I had noticed that while we were standing on the train. Now she was slightly taller, because we'd started up the stairs and she was a step above me.

Even once we'd reached the waiting room, she didn't look around. Thirtieth Street Station is so enormous and echoing and high-ceilinged—a jolt after cozy Baltimore—that most people pause to take stock a moment, but not Sophia. She just went clicking along, with me a few yards to the rear.

At the Information island, only one person stood waiting. I spotted her from far across those acres of marble flooring: a girl in a denim jacket and jeans, with a billow of crinkly, electric red hair. It fanned straight out and stopped just above her shoulders. It was *amazing* hair. I was awestruck. Sophia, though, didn't let on she had noticed her. She was walking more slowly now, downright sedately, placing her toes at a slight angle outward, the way women often do when they want to look composed and genteel. Actually, she was starting to get on my nerves. Didn't that bun of hers just sum her up, I thought— the net that bound it in and the perfect, doughnut shape and the way it sat so low on her head, so matronly and drab! And Esther Brimm, meanwhile, stood burning like a candle on her stick-thin, blue-denim legs.

When we reached the island I veered right, toward a display of schedules on the counter. I heard Sophia's heels stop in front of Esther. "Esther Brimm?" she asked.

"Ms. Maynard?"

Husky, throaty voice, the kind I like.

"Your father asked me to bring you something. . . ."

I took a schedule from the rack and turned my face casually in their direction. Not till Esther said, "Right; my passport," did Sophia slip the mailer from behind her book and hold it out.

"Thanks a million," Esther said, accepting it, and Sophia said, "My pleasure. Have a good trip." Then she turned away and clicked toward the Twenty-ninth Street exit.

Just like that, I forgot her. Now I was focused on Esther. *Open it!* I told her. Instead she picked up the army duffel lying at her feet and moved off toward the phones. I meandered after her, studying my schedule. I pretended I was hunting a train to Princeton.

The phones were the unprivate kind just out in the middle of everything, standing cheek to jowl. When Esther lifted a receiver off its hook, I was right there beside her, lifting a receiver of my own. I was so near I could have touched her duffel bag with the toe of my sneaker. I heard every word she said. "Dad?" she said.

I clamped my phone to my ear and held the schedule up between us so I could watch her. This close, she was less attractive. She had that fragile, sore-looking skin you often find on redheads. "Yes," she was saying, "it's here." And then, "Sure! I guess so. I mean, it's still stapled shut and all. Huh? Well, hang on "

She put her receiver down and started yanking at the mailer's top flap. When the staples tore loose, rat-a-tat, she pulled the edges apart and peered inside—practically stuck her little freckled nose inside. Then she picked up the phone again. "Yup," she said. "Good as new."

So I never got a chance to see for myself. It could have been anything: loose diamonds, crack cocaine . . . But somehow I didn't think so. The phone call was what convinced me. She'd have had to be a criminal genius to fake that careless tone of voice, the easy offhandedness of a person who knows for a fact that she's her parents' pride and joy. "Well, listen," she was saying. "Tell Mom I'll call again from the airport, okay?" And she made a kissing sound and hung up. When she slung her duffel over her shoulder and started toward one of the gates, I didn't even watch her go.

Anne Tyler was born in Minneapolis in 1941 but grew up in Raleigh, North Carolina. She graduated at nineteen from Duke University, and went on to do graduate work in Russian studies at Columbia University. Her eleventh novel, *Breathing Lessons,* was awarded the Pulitzer Prize in 1988. Tyler is a member of the American Academy of Arts and Letters. She lives in Baltimore.

THE UMBRELLA COUNTRY

Bino A. Realuyo

Dear BRC Reader,

When I first read *The Umbrella Country*, I was swept away by the beauty of its language, the poignancy of its story, and the varied shadings of its characters and settings. This story of 1970s Manila—as much about America as it is the Philippines—is told by eleven-year-old Gringo, an acutely sensitive boy who becomes the hub of a family wheel spinning out of control.

When the story starts, Gringo's life is still steeped in childhood innocence and games, and the first part of the book follows his naivete while giving glimpses of the storms to come. In the second part there is much turmoil and growing pains as Gringo's godmother, Ninang Rola, confides to him that his older brother, Pipo, was born of rape and that their mother, Estrella, never wanted to marry Daddy Groovie but had no choice. He stands by helplessly as Pipo and Estrella are beaten for the smallest of reasons, but mainly because their presence reminds Daddy Groovie of the dead end he's made of his life. Eventually the whole family goes flying apart and is only saved by Daddy Groovie getting his papers and moving to Nuyork.

The third part takes on a new menace in the wake of Daddy Groovie's departure: Pipo is brutally raped, and the rapist is murdered, while Gringo lets their mother believe that it was he that suffered. As the family prepares to follow Daddie Groovie to the States, Gringo faces the greatest tragedy of his life—and prevails.

Amy Scheibe
Editor

Miss Unibers

A bird died at the first sign of flooding.

From our second-story window, I could connect all forms of destruction with a seasonal song while I watched our neighbors fill up Tupperware, buckets, and drums with rain to be carried inside, but still, we quietly resisted the rain. The higher the flood rose, the more lives it took, sometimes animals—rats, dogs, frogs—floated in the flood and sometimes people and homes, which I had not seen myself but heard so much about. It was only this time of the year when I felt that there was more than enough of anything for everybody. As long as I could remember, water has always been scarce; it often got cut off or dripped out of the faucets. Not that I looked forward to floods because most of that type of water we couldn't use anyway, but the sight of water gushing out of nowhere always reminded me that somebody up there understood what was lacking down here.

A quick slam of wind pushed me away from the window, closer to Pipo who was on the floor beside his Miss Unibers box.

"What are you going to wear this time?" I asked, when I saw him cutting little crescent moon shaped pictures out of magazines. No answer. I could only hear the gush of humming rain outside and murmurs of little children as they playfully chanted over the death of the little Maya bird, slowly being whirled into the sewer.

Meanwhile, Pipo studied a black-and-white picture he had taken from Mommy awhile back. Although he never asked me to watch the door or listen to approaching voices and footsteps, I would always stand guard whenever he did this, so nobody could suddenly walk up the stairs and catch him.

"Are you wearing *that*?"

Miss Unibers, our game of the season.

Games appeared and disappeared in our street. When they came back, if they ever did, they would usually take another form, like soft drink bottle caps: gambled with one year, shot up into the gutters the next, and flattened to become caroling instruments at Christmas. It happened every few months to accommodate the changing weather, but no one could really tell what we would come up with next. Unpredictable as typhoons, *pabago-bago ng isip*, the elders would say about us because our temperaments changed quickly, sometimes long after a flood or before all our rubber slippers were made into boats.

While all the other boys gambled with marbles, playcards, and rubber bands to know who would be ruling our street next, the rest of us busied ourselves with Miss Unibers in those last days of the sun. I remember it clearly: I was standing at the back of the red cement steps of English-speaking Titay's verandah, watching with dismay the two contestants left in front of us. Plants in big terra cotta pots made leafy walls on either side of the stairs and the big, old wooden doors carved with the letter *R*. We were hidden from outside, from other children like Big Boy Jun and his marble-gambling friends who would surely taunt us upon seeing us in costumes. The tall plants absorbed our voices, even English-speaking Titay's loud, cracking one.

"Secon-runnerup, Miss Germanee!" Her voice was an out-of-tune song.

I clapped my hands to a succession of questions, overlapping like the rat-tat-tat yells of newspaper boys in the morning. Why was everybody so quiet when I sang? Would I ever make it to the top three? Did I have to sneak out in my mother's clothes to win this? Wasn't a wraparound of bed sheets and curtains enough for a gown?

"Firs-runnerup, Miss Ha-why."

English-speaking Titay gingerly pinned the sequined sash around Ling-ling who was wearing her first holy communion dress, layered with lace. English-speaking Titay was known for harassing boys with her big, flabby arms and her English in such a way that nobody would engage her in an altercation, mistaking the thickness of her skin for English proficiency. "What chu want?" she yelled at a boy one time, and the boy ran away, frightened not by English-speaking Titay, who was shorter than him, but by words he couldn't understand.

I fingered the edge of my glittering sash as I gawked at the plastic table roses stuck across Ling-ling's chest, the green stems visible from afar. I had thought about wearing something similar but I couldn't find any in our house. We had only kept real plants; cutting parts of them would probably kill them. Ninang Rola would certainly get upset, especially after having patiently spent a great deal of time applying egg white on the leaves for them to glimmer. I grabbed my falling wraparound, wondering what had happened to the big safety pin that kept my costume in place. "Stop wiggling." Ling-ling turned to me with huge eyes and a whisper while she faked a smile on her face. Born a duck, she grew up into a girl. But even at the age of nine, she still possessed all the characteristics of a duck: her toes were so spread open that pebbles would always get caught between them; she lifted one leg to rest; her tongue was too small, she squeaked when she spoke.

"Tenk chu. Tenk chu. Eeek."

The winner stood there, towering over all of us. Unlike me, he hardly had a spot of sweat on his face. His costume was an island spice, flavored with candlewax fruits on his head and a very, very tight nightgown, the one Mommy had been looking for for over a month. For days, she attached *puñeta* to all the names of our closest relatives—*puñeta* Mrs.-from-across-the-street, *puñeta* Sgt. Dragon Dimaculangan, *puñeta* Baby Cherry Pie—blaming the neighbors for stealing our clothesline with fishhooks. I never said a word. I wasn't even surprised to see Mommy's nightgown appear again as a gown with heart-shaped pieces of velvet fabric pasted all over it, shoulder straps replaced by a plastic vine of sequined multicolored leaves, a lace table runner on his back like a cape. All of them looking familiar. Even him. Pipo. Miss Unibers.

For the third time.

The rain swooshed so heavily that the sliding window shutters almost shook out of their grooves. I held them firmly to keep them from falling over. Behind me was Pipo. Behind me, our room. Pipo. This room layered with wallpaper over the years. Mommy said I was born here. In this very space, a few months after Pipo was born, I was conceived. It could have been raining outside, too; that was when couples like Sgt. and Mrs. Dimaculangan had nothing better to do but make babies. It could have been during the summer, during one of the brownout nights, when the city tried to conserve energy and turned everybody's lights off. Those nights, when mosquitoes haloed people's heads, they slid the shutters close. Then I was conceived. Then I was born.

There was one big bed in the middle of our room.

Mommy and Daddy Groovie slept there, where I could have been conceived but no one would say. They never spoke to me about things that happened before my birth as if our lives only began thereafter. When I looked at the bed, I always imagined Mommy and Daddy Groovie's cockfight at night, thinking I could have been conceived immediately after what they did. That same bed was where I spent mornings as a small child waking up in my own wetness. Mommy covered the mattress with a multifold of blankets because of the stains I left. She decided one day to stuff my Jockeys with thick pieces of carefully folded cloth so that when I wet at night, I wouldn't wet the bed. I would go to sleep with a huge bulge in my shorts. Every morning when I woke up, the cloth was soaking wet. And so was the bed. A bigger wet spot overlapping with the other stains. Mommy said I would ruin the bed by peeing on it all the time, so she decided to move us into a bunk, me on top, Pipo on the bottom. The mattresses were thin. In a few months, they were thinner. The following year, I stopped wetting myself. I dreamt that I was inside an empty drum that we used to fill with rainwater. Somehow, being inside, the drum was taller than me. The paint inside peeled. It began to rain. Not until the rain reached my neck did I realize it was my own pee. Boy Manicure, from the beauty parlor five houses away, was there. Although I couldn't see him, I knew he was watching and laughing away. It could have been the sound of his laughter that reverberated inside the drum that woke me up, or the sudden flash of his technicolor Revlon face in front of me. But I knew when I woke up I was dry, and I had been waking up dry since. I told everybody that a dream of rain healed me. Ninang Rola attributed the change to God's blessings, which for her, and many of us, came through rain from above.

* * *

A window in a house. A big open eye that never slept.

The same window where Daddy Groovie spent his days sitting, watching the movement of life outside while he chewed on his peanuts. He would wilt like guava leaves on a hot summer day, collecting his dreams of the States, putting them in little heaps the way he would peanut shells. Sometimes, the wind would blow his peanut shells and Pipo and I would catch them like falling yellow leaves. Once, he created paper boats that never sank in the flood. He must have seen Pipo and me struggling with little boats made of paper, cardboard, or rubber slippers. He taught us how to make them. I was seven then. Another moment with Daddy Groovie worth putting in a picture album because it was never to happen again. While it rained outside, Daddy Groovie taught us how to fold the paper differently, what edges to cut, and once the boat was done, where to prop it up with a popsicle stick so that it wouldn't sink. He would say over and over again how lucky we were to learn this from him since his own father never taught him anything, how there were certain things we had to discover ourselves. While Pipo built the paper boat himself, I was imagining how many black ants I could put in the boat. I lost one of the paper boats one day; when I found it again, it was still floating on the flood, resting on a stone, the ants very safe inside. At times, we would put black and red ants together in one boat and see what they would do to each other while floating on the flood. Nothing. They just made little holes on the paper.

Little windows on a boat.

Pipo would never give up. "Could paper planes fly better?" He once handed Daddy Groovie a plane he had just made. Daddy Groovie took it from his hands, watched it fly into a curve, go into the back of the cabinet and disappear. "Now you know," was Daddy Groovie's response while he walked away laughing. "What do you think of that, *PanAm*?" Pipo attempted again a few times—a house made of popsicle sticks, a sword made of bamboo, the proper way to turn slippers into boats. Each time Daddy Groovie ignored him, saying, "About time for you to learn this yourself." Since then, Pipo learned to discover all on his own, houses in shoeboxes, paint in nail polish, dresses in curtains. He learned to use his hands, sometimes acquiring Daddy Groovie's heavy hands, chasing me with them, hitting me right on the head, my back, or using them to throw things that he could never improve: a tilting cardboard that was supposed to be a choo-choo train, a wornout slipper sliced in half to be a boat, a shoebox dripping with nail polish that could have been a newly polished doll house, and a Miss Unibers nightgown ripped in the middle.

Soon rain became the rhythm of humming, creating so many different sounds, so many songs for this flooded city. The thickness of the season lay on the ground, at least ankle-high. People sang or whistled while they plodded through the flood. I could hear little children singing for the sun to come back. Radios were on, alternating between early morning love songs and weather news updates.

Inside our bedroom, I repeatedly hummed a song I sang at our Miss Unibers. I could still hear the enveloping silence when I delivered my bathroom-rehearsed talent. Nobody looked at me. It would have been better if they laughed or expressed some form of emotion so that I could know how bad I was. I knew I couldn't sing and didn't have any other talent. Just this round, owl-eyed face. Twin balloons for cheeks as if I were always keeping air inside my mouth, about to blow Juicy Fruit. Lower lips protruding so that one could see the soft flesh inside, a mouth of pouting, a mouth that always seemed to cry. Gaps between chipped teeth, so that whenever I saw a Colgate commercial I felt that everybody was looking at me, up and down, my mouth getting smaller and smaller, this giant toothbrush attacking me.

My face was similar to the dark, except night became day and my face stayed the same. Many times, I had attempted to transform it by smiling differently, masking it behind daydreams of beauty queens in the black-and-white pictures Mommy kept from the sixties. Long glittering gowns. Mesmerizing bouffant hairdos. Arms and fingers, bent and spread out like mannequins in eternal postures of display, or like Virgen Maria on church pedestals, rings of flowers curling around her fingers, every week a new one. I imagined I was the mannequin at Aling Tina's tailor shop at the end of our street, whose dress changed every week. I would have the long and light-colored hair of Delilah de Samsona, the mannequin at Boy Manicure's beauty parlor. The perfect angular face of Sonja Carolina Santa Cruz, the head of a mannequin that mysteriously appeared and disappeared on Mommy's decade old Singer machine. But somehow I always ended up looking plain and flat, and my costumes like the old blankets that Mommy dressed the ironing board with.

And the one who managed to come up with the best costumes was the same one who secretly stole Sonja Carolina Santa Cruz's mannequin head to use for fitting his hairpieces, kept his Miss Unibers box under the bunk bed. But deep inside me, I knew that he was born with the ability to turn towels and bedsheets into the most decorative gowns, and to walk with grace on his long legs without bending his back or losing his balance. *That* I could never quite get right. I didn't have the gift of long legs. Towels hung lifeless around my neck. I never thought about wrapping them around my head, the way Pipo did all the time, even at home. At our first Miss Unibers, he capped his head with Mommy's floral towel, a huge hairpiece, with all the flowers decoratively showing, and so high, twice the size of his head! He became Miss Kodak. Miss Swimsuit. Miss Long Gown. And eventually, Miss Unibers.

Born and raised in Manila, BINO REALUYO studied International Relations in the U.S. and South America. He has also completed a poetry collection, *In Spite of Open Eyes*, and is currently editing *The NuyorAsian Anthology*, a collection of Asian American writings about New York City. He is published widely in literary journals and anthologies both in the U.S. and the Philippines, including *The Kenyon Review, Manoa, New Letters, The Literary Review,* and *Likhaan: Best of Philippine Poetry.*

A Widow for One Year

John Irving

Dear BRC Reader,

Twenty years after *The World According to Garp*, John Irving gives us a new novel about a family marked by tragedy.

Ruth Cole is a complex, often self-contradictory character—a "difficult" woman. By no means is she conventionally "nice," but she will never be forgotten.

Ruth's story is told in three parts, each focusing on a critical time in her life. When we first meet her—on Long Island, in the summer of 1958—Ruth is only four.

The second window into Ruth's life opens on the fall of 1990, when Ruth is an unmarried woman whose personal life is not nearly as successful as her literary career. She distrusts her judgment in men, for good reason.

A Widow for One Year closes in the autumn of 1995, when Ruth Cole is a forty-one-year-old widow and mother. She's about to fall in love for the first time.

Richly comic, as well as deeply disturbing, *A Widow for One Year* is a multilayered love story of astonishing emotional force. Both ribald and erotic, it is also a brilliant novel about the passage of time and the relentlessness of grief

Linda Grey
President

The Inadequate Lamp Shade

One night when she was four and sleeping in the bottom bunk of her bunk bed, Ruth Cole woke to the sound of lovemaking—it was coming from her parents' bedroom. It was a totally unfamiliar sound to her. Ruth had recently been ill with a stomach flu; when she first heard her mother making love, Ruth thought that her mother was throwing up.

It was not as simple a matter as her parents having separate bedrooms; that summer they had separate houses, although Ruth never saw the other house. Her parents spent alternate nights in the family house with Ruth; there was a rental house nearby, where Ruth's mother or father stayed when they weren't staying with Ruth. It was one of those ridiculous arrangements that couples make when they are separating, but before they are divorced—when they still imagine that children and property can be shared with more magnanimity than recrimination.

When Ruth woke to the foreign sound, she at first wasn't sure if it was her mother or her father who was throwing up; then, despite the unfamiliarity of the disturbance, Ruth recognized that measure of melancholy and contained hysteria which was often detectable in her mother's voice. Ruth also remembered that it was her mother's turn to stay with her.

The master bathroom separated Ruth's room from the master bedroom. When the four-year-old padded barefoot through the bathroom, she took a towel with her. (When she'd been sick with the stomach flu, her father had encouraged her to vomit in a towel.) Poor Mommy! Ruth thought, bringing her the towel.

In the dim moonlight, and in the even dimmer and erratic light from the night-light that Ruth's father had installed in the bathroom, Ruth saw the pale faces of her dead brothers in the photographs on the bathroom wall. There were photos of her dead brothers throughout the house, on all the walls; although the two boys had died as teenagers, before Ruth was born (before she was even conceived), Ruth felt that she knew these vanished young men far better than she knew her mother or father.

The tall, dark one with the angular face was Thomas; even at Ruth's age, when he'd been only four, Thomas had had a leading man's kind of handsomeness—a combination of poise and thuggery that, in his teenage years, gave him the seeming confidence of a much older man. (Thomas had been the driver of the doomed car.)

The younger, insecure-looking one was Timothy; even as a teenager, he was baby-faced and appeared to have just been startled by something. In many of the photographs, Timothy seemed to be caught in a moment of indecision, as if he were perpetually reluctant to imitate an incredibly difficult stunt that Thomas had mastered with apparent ease. (In the end, it was something as basic as driving a car that Thomas failed to master sufficiently.)

When Ruth Cole entered her parents' bedroom, she saw the naked young man who had mounted her mother from behind; he was holding her mother's breasts in his hands and humping her on all fours, like a dog, but it was neither the violence nor the repugnance of the sexual act that caused Ruth to scream. The four-year-old didn't know that she was witnessing a sexual act—nor did the young man and her mother's activity strike Ruth as entirely unpleasant. In fact, Ruth was relieved to see that her mother was *not* throwing up.

And it wasn't the young man's nakedness that caused Ruth to scream; she had seen her father and her mother naked—nakedness was not hidden among the Coles. It was the young man himself who made Ruth scream, because she was certain he was one of her dead brothers; he looked so much like Thomas, the confident one, that Ruth Cole believed she had seen a ghost.

A four-year-old's scream is a piercing sound. Ruth was astonished at the speed with which her mother's young lover dismounted;

indeed, he removed himself from both the woman and her bed with such a combination of panic and zeal that he appeared to be *propelled*—it was almost as if a cannonball had dislodged him. He fell over the night table, and, in an effort to conceal his nakedness, removed the lamp shade from the broken bedside lamp. As such, he seemed a less menacing sort of ghost than Ruth had first judged him to be; furthermore, now that Ruth took a closer look at him, she recognized him. He was the boy who occupied the most distant guest room, the boy who drove her father's car—the boy who worked for her daddy, her mommy had said. Once or twice the boy had driven Ruth and her babysitter to the beach.

That summer, Ruth had three different nannies; each of them had commented on how pale the boy was, but Ruth's mother had told her that some people just didn't like the sun. The child had never before seen the boy without his clothes, of course; yet Ruth was certain that the young man's name was Eddie and that he *wasn't* a ghost. Nevertheless, the four-year-old screamed again.

Her mother, still on all fours on her bed, looked characteristically unsurprised; she merely viewed her daughter with an expression of discouragement edged with despair. Before Ruth could cry out a third time, her mother said, "Don't scream, honey. It's just Eddie and me. Go back to bed."

Ruth Cole did as she was told, once more passing those photographs—more ghostly-seeming now than her mother's fallen ghost of a lover. Eddie, while attempting to hide himself with the lamp shade, had been oblivious to the fact that the lamp shade, being open at both ends, afforded Ruth an unobstructed view of his diminishing penis.

At four, Ruth was too young to ever remember Eddie *or* his penis with the greatest detail, but he would remember her. Thirty-six years later, when he was fifty-two and Ruth was forty, this ill-fated young man would fall in love with Ruth Cole. Yet not even then would he regret having fucked Ruth's mother. Alas, that would be Eddie's problem. This is Ruth's story.

That her parents had expected her to be a third son was not the reason Ruth Cole became a writer; a more likely source of her imagination was that she grew up in a house where the photographs of her dead brothers were a stronger presence than any "presence" she detected in either her mother or her father—and that, after her mother abandoned her *and* her father (and took with her almost *all* the photos of her lost sons), Ruth would wonder why her father left the picture hooks stuck in the bare walls. The picture hooks were part of the reason she became a writer—for years after her mother left, Ruth would try to remember which of the photographs had hung from which of the hooks. And, failing to recall the actual pictures of her perished brothers to her satisfaction, Ruth began to invent all the captured moments in their short lives, which she had missed. That Thomas and Timothy were killed before she was born was another part of the reason Ruth Cole became a writer; from her earliest memory, she was forced to imagine them.

It was one of those automobile accidents involving teenagers that, in the aftermath, revealed that both boys had been "good kids" and that neither of them had been drinking. Worst of all, to the endless torment of their parents, the coincidence of Thomas and Timothy being in that car at that exact time, and in that specific place, was the result of an altogether avoidable quarrel between the boys' mother and father. The poor parents would relive the tragic results of their trivial argument for the rest of their lives.

Later Ruth was told that she was conceived in a well-intentioned but passionless act. Ruth's parents were mistaken to even imagine that their sons were replaceable—nor did they pause to consider that the new baby who would bear the burden of their impossible expectations might be a *girl*.

That Ruth Cole would grow up to be that rare combination of a well-respected literary novelist *and* an internationally best-selling author is not as remarkable as the fact that she managed to grow up at all. Those handsome young men in the photographs had stolen most of her mother's affection; however, her mother's rejection was more bearable to Ruth than growing up in the shadow of the coldness that passed between her parents.

Ted Cole, a best-selling author and illustrator of books for children, was a handsome man who was better at writing and drawing for children than he was at fulfilling the daily responsibilities of fatherhood. And until Ruth was four-and-a-half, while Ted Cole was not always drunk, he frequently drank too much. It's also true that, while Ted was not a womanizer every waking minute, at no time in his life was he ever entirely *not* a womanizer. (Granted, this made him more unreliable with women than he was with children.)

Ted had ended up writing for children by default. His literary debut was an overpraised adult novel of an indisputably literary sort. The two novels that followed aren't worth mentioning, except to say that no one—especially Ted Cole's publisher—had expressed any noticeable interest in a fourth novel, which was never written. Instead, Ted wrote his first children's book. Called *The Mouse Crawling Between the Walls*, it was very nearly not published; at first glance, it appeared to be one of those children's books that are of dubious appeal to parents and remain memorable to children only because children remember being frightened. At least Thomas and Timothy were frightened by *The Mouse Crawling Between the Walls* when Ted first told them the story; by the time Ted told it to Ruth, *The Mouse Crawling Between the Walls* had already frightened about nine or ten million children, in more than thirty languages, around the world.

Like her dead brothers, Ruth grew up on her father's stories. When Ruth first read these stories in a book, it felt like a violation of her privacy. She'd imagined that her father had created these stories for her alone. Later she would wonder if her dead brothers had felt that *their* privacy had been similarly invaded.

Regarding Ruth's mother: Marion Cole was a beautiful woman; she was also a good mother, at least until Ruth was born. And until the deaths of her beloved sons, she was a loyal and faithful wife—despite her husband's countless infidelities. But after the accident that took her boys away, Marion became a different woman, distant and cold. Because of her apparent indifference to her daughter, Marion was relatively easy for Ruth to reject. It would be harder for Ruth to recognize what was flawed about her father; it would also take a lot longer for her to come to this recognition, and by then it would be too late for Ruth to turn completely against him. Ted had charmed her—Ted charmed almost everyone, up to a certain age. No one was ever charmed by Marion. Poor Marion never tried to charm anyone, not even her only daughter; yet it was possible to *love* Marion Cole.

And this is where Eddie, the unlucky young man with the inadequate lamp shade, enters the story. *He* loved Marion—he would never stop loving her. Naturally if he'd known from the beginning that he was going to fall in love with Ruth, he might have reconsidered falling in love with her mother. But probably not. Eddie couldn't help himself.

Summer Job

His name was Edward O'Hare. In the summer of 1958, he had recently turned sixteen—having his driver's license had been a prerequisite of his first summer job. But Eddie O'Hare was unaware that becoming Marion Cole's lover would turn out to be his *real* summer job; Ted Cole had hired him specifically for this reason, and it would have lifelong results.

Eddie had heard of the tragedy in the Cole family, but—as with most teenagers—his attention to adult conversation was sporadic. He'd completed his second year at Phillips Exeter Academy, where his father taught English; it was an Exeter connection that got Eddie the job. Eddie's father ebulliently believed in Exeter connections. First a graduate of the academy and then a faculty member, the senior O'Hare never took a vacation without his well-thumbed copy of the *Exeter Directory*. In his view, the alumni of the academy were the standard-bearers of an ongoing responsibility—Exonians trusted one another, and they did favors for one another when they could.

In the view of the academy, the Coles had already been generous to Exeter. Their doomed sons were successful and popular students at the school when they died; despite their grief, or probably because of it, Ted and Marion Cole had funded an annual visiting lecturer in English literature—Thomas and Timothy's best subject. "Minty" O'Hare, as the senior O'Hare was known to countless Exeter students, was addicted to breath mints, which he lovingly sucked while reading aloud in class; he was inordinately fond of reciting his favorite passages from the books he'd assigned. The so-called Thomas and Timothy Cole Lectures had been Minty O'Hare's idea.

And when Eddie had expressed to his father that his first choice for a summer job would be to work as an assistant to a *writer*—the sixteen-year-old had long kept a diary and had recently written some short stories—the senior O'Hare hadn't hesitated to consult his *Exeter Directory*. To be sure, there were many more *literary* writers than Ted Cole among the alumni—Thomas and Timothy had gone to Exeter because Ted was an alumnus—but Minty O'Hare, who had managed only four years earlier to persuade Ted Cole to part with $82,000, knew that Ted was an easy touch.

"You don't have to pay him anything to speak of," Minty told Ted on the telephone. "The boy could type things for you, or answer letters, run errands—whatever you want. It's mainly for the experience.

I mean, if he thinks he wants to be a writer, he should see how one works."

On the phone, Ted was noncommittal but polite; he was also drunk. He had his own name for Minty O'Hare—Ted called him "Pushy." And, indeed, it was typical of Pushy O'Hare that he pointed out the whereabouts of Eddie's photographs in the 1957 *PEAN* (the Exeter yearbook).

For the first few years after the deaths of Thomas and Timothy Cole, Marion had requested Exeter yearbooks. Had he lived, Thomas would have graduated with the class of '54—Timothy, in '56. But now, every year, even past their would-be graduations, the yearbooks came—courtesy of Minty O'Hare, who sent them automatically, assuming that he was sparing Marion the additional suffering of asking for them. Marion continued to look them over faithfully; she was repeatedly struck by those boys who bore any resemblance to Thomas or Timothy, although she'd stopped indicating these resemblances to Ted after Ruth was born.

In the pages of the '57 *PEAN*, Eddie O'Hare is seated in the front row in the photograph of the Junior Debating Society; in his dark-gray flannel trousers, tweed jacket, regimental-striped tie, he would have been nondescript except for an arresting frankness in his expression and the solemn anticipation of some future sorrow in his large, dark eyes.

In the picture, Eddie was two years younger than Thomas and the same age as Timothy at the time of their deaths. Nevertheless, Eddie looked more like Thomas than like Timothy; he looked even *more* like Thomas in the photo of the Outing Club, where Eddie appeared more clear skinned and confident than the majority of those other boys who possessed what Ted Cole assumed was an abiding interest in the outdoors. Eddie's only other appearances in the '57 Exeter yearbook were in the photographs of two junior-varsity athletic teams—J.V. Cross-Country and J.V. Track. Eddie's leanness suggested that the boy ran more out of nervousness than for any apparent pleasure, and that running might possibly be his only athletic inclination.

It was with feigned casualness that Ted Cole showed these pictures of young Edward O'Hare to his wife. "This boy looks a lot like Thomas, doesn't he?" he asked.

Marion had seen the photographs before; she'd looked at all the photos in all the Exeter yearbooks very closely. "Yes, somewhat," she replied. "Why? Who is he?"

"He wants a summer job," Ted told her.

"With *us*?"

"Well, with *me*," Ted said. "He wants to be a writer."

"But what would he do with you?" Marion asked.

"It's mainly for the experience, I suppose," Ted told her. "I mean, if he thinks he wants to be a writer, he should see how one works."

Marion, who'd always had aspirations of being a writer herself, knew that her husband didn't work very much. "But what exactly would he *do*?" she asked.

"Well." Ted had a habit of leaving his sentences and thoughts unfinished, incomplete. It was both a deliberate and an unconscious part of his vagueness.

When he called back Minty O'Hare to offer his son a job, Ted's first question was whether Eddie had his driver's license. Ted had suffered his second drunk-driving conviction and was without a driver's license for the summer of '58. He'd hoped that the summer might be a good time to initiate a so-called trial separation from Marion, but if he were to rent a house nearby, and yet continue to share the family house (and Ruth) with Marion, someone would have to drive him.

"Certainly he has his license!" Minty told Ted. Thus was the boy's fate sealed.

And so Marion's question regarding what Eddie O'Hare would *do*, exactly, was left standing in the manner that Ted Cole frequently let things stand—namely, he let things stand vaguely. He also left Marion sitting with the Exeter yearbook open in her lap; he often left her that way. He couldn't help noticing that Marion seemed to find the photograph of Eddie O'Hare in his track uniform the most riveting. With the long, pink nail of her index finger, Marion was tracing the borders of Eddie's bare shoulders; it was an unconscious but intensely focused gesture. Ted had to wonder if *he* wasn't more aware of his wife's increasing obsession with boys who resembled Thomas or Timothy than poor Marion was. After all, she hadn't slept with one of them yet.

Eddie would be the only one she *would* sleep with.

© COOK NEILSON

JOHN WINSLOW IRVING was born in Exeter, New Hampshire, in 1942. He is the author of nine novels, among them *The World According to Garp, The Hotel New Hampshire, The Cider House Rules, A Prayer for Owen Meany,* and *A Son of the Circus.* Mr. Irving is married and has three sons; he lives in Toronto and in southern Vermont.

THE HUNGER MOON

Suzanne Matson

Dear BRC Reader,

Hunger Moon is a beautifully crafted debut novel that follows the inter-connected lives of three very different women, bound forever by chance and circumstance. Renata is a single mother who, after keeping her pregnancy and baby boy a secret from the sweet but troubled fa-ther, flees California in an adventurous drive across the country. She ends up staying in Boston, where she finds work waitressing. She soon meets her next-door neighbor, Eleanor, an elegant, 78-year-old widow. After recently moving out of the house where she and her family resided for over fifty years, Eleanor now lives alone in a stark apart-ment populated with unpacked boxes. June, an anorexic/bulimic dance student with an unhappy childhood, does odd jobs for Eleanor to make extra money. The lives of the three women become interwoven as they come together to take turns looking after Charlie, Renata's baby. We love this novel not only for the irresistibly moving tribute to the unique relationships between women, themselves, and the men who love them—but also for Matson's sensitive but not sentimental, lyrical yet crisp telling. Matson, who is also a poet, subtly captures the very recognizable rhythm of life, ensuring a thoroughly engaging read and, undoubtedly, a very bright literary future ahead of her.

This excerpt illustrates the beginning of the blossoming friendship between the three women. Through baby talk and bonding over Char-lie, Renata, Eleanor, and June slowly begin to reveal bits of themselves to one another. Matson's delicate prose captures the essence of the women as they become acquainted, these likeable, everyday women whose concerns, problems, triumphs, and joys are reflections of our own.

Maureen O'Neal
Editorial Director,
Trade Paperbacks

June

When Mrs. M. buzzed her in, the older woman had a look of excitement about her, almost bordering on gaiety. "I have a surprise for you today, June."

June had never seen her this way, almost girlish.

"We're having a visitor, and I promised that you would help me entertain him."

"Him? Are you expecting a gentleman caller, Mrs. MacGregor?"

"You'll have to wait. They're not expected for another half hour, so you must stay in suspense while you do the vacuuming."

As June tidied up the apartment, she noticed that the Christmas lights were on. They glowed against the puddles of melting snow on the deck.

At one-thirty there was a knock on the apartment door. Mrs. MacGregor opened it and admitted Renata and Charlie.

"June, I believe you've already met my new neighbors. Renata has an appointment to keep at two, so you and I will be in charge of entertaining young Charlie. Are we equal to it?"

"Sure. How are you?" June greeted Renata, then went up to the baby and shook his sock-encased toe.

Charlie stared at her balefully.

"He just woke up from a nap, so he's a little fuzzy still. I'm afraid that means he'll be awake the whole time for you."

"That's good news for us, isn't it, June?"

June had never seen Mrs. MacGregor so animated. Renata and Mrs. M. both seemed to be expecting June to make some move. "Will he let me hold him?" June asked skeptically.

Renata handed Charlie to her, and June was surprised at the baby's dense weight. He seemed content to examine her face. "How old is Charlie?" she asked.

"Almost five months."

June had never been around babies much, so she didn't know if this one was an advanced specimen or not. But she figured that mothers always liked to hear that their offspring were thriving. "He's big," she told Renata.

"Isn't he? We went to the pediatrician yesterday, and found out that he's already sixteen pounds."

"Oh, that is big. What was he at birth?" Mrs. MacGregor asked.

"Only seven-two."

Mrs. M. and Renata talked baby stats for the next five minutes. Surprisingly, Mrs. M. knew the weights and lengths of her three children not only at birth but at several points during their first two years. June had never understood the fascination with these figures, but then it occurred to her that some people might not care how many calories were in a slice of honeydew melon either, one of approximately seven or eight hundred nutritional values she held in storage in her brain.

"Will he be getting hungry?" Mrs. MacGregor asked.

"I don't think so. I fed him before bringing him over. But just in case, I have a little bit of milk that I expressed." Renata fished inside the diaper bag for a bottle. "I was thinking about what we talked about—how he's never been with a baby-sitter yet. And I realized Charlie's never had to drink from a bottle. Not once. Can you believe that never occurred to me before?"

Mrs. MacGregor nodded sympathetically. "Well, you wouldn't think of it if you didn't need him to take a bottle, now, would you?"

"I don't know what I was thinking. He'll need to have a baby-sitter when I go back to work. Anyway, I went out and got one of those pumps—I don't know if you've seen them—and expressed some breast milk to give him myself from a bottle."

"And?"

"He wasn't crazy about it. I had to kind of pace back and forth while I gave it to him, and he kept looking at me like I was nuts the whole time, didn't you, Charlie?"

Charlie was sitting on June's knee, staring at his mother's face.

"But he did take it. And I did the same thing yesterday, so if he does need a bottle today, he should know what to do with it. I'll be back soon enough that he probably won't even get hungry, though."

Renata showed them the disposable diapers and wipes in the bag, and Mrs. MacGregor marveled at how everything had gotten so much more practical since her day.

"You just run along to your appointment, and we'll be fine, won't we, June?"

"Of course we will. I think he likes me." Charlie had swiveled his head now from his mother to June. After studying her for a minute, he decided to smile.

"Okay. I know he'll be fine." Renata didn't seem to know what to do. She kissed the top of Charlie's head, and shifted uncertainly.

Mrs. MacGregor finally ushered her to the door. "You'll be late. And I wouldn't want you to be rushed. Salons are meant to be enjoyed."

"Thank you, Eleanor. I'll be back soon. Be good, Charlie."

Charlie stared at his mother's departing back and then at the door that closed behind her.

"Well, now," June said, shifting him around to look at her. "You were a good surprise," she told him.

"I thought you'd be pleased," said Mrs. MacGregor. "You've watched babies before, haven't you?"

"Never," June said.

"Oh."

They looked at each other and laughed.

"Well," said Mrs. MacGregor, "I have. Not in a while, of course. Though I don't expect babies have changed much since I had them. You can be the brawn in this operation and I'll be the brains."

"Well, thank you very much."

Just then Charlie decided to spit up part of his feeding. June dashed to the kitchen for a dishtowel while Mrs. MacGregor dug through the diaper bag for a burp cloth. June wiped the front of the baby and her arm, while Mrs. MacGregor saw to the couch. "I had forgotten about that," Mrs. M. said.

Charlie looked from June's face to Mrs. MacGregor's and his lower lip began to quiver. In a few seconds he tightened his eyes to slits and began to cry.

"What do we do now?" June said, jiggling him.

"Oh, dear. You were such a happy little boy when I saw you last," Mrs. MacGregor told him.

June paced. Mrs. MacGregor walked beside her, jingling keys and shaking the brightly colored dishcloth. Charlie howled. June shifted him to a new position over her shoulder, and in the process of being moved Charlie released a large burp.

"Well," they said together.

Charlie grinned.

Mrs. MacGregor held him on the couch while June spread a blanket on the floor and put out some toys Renata had brought over. Then she put him on his back and sat beside him, putting the toys in his hands one by one. He brought each one to his mouth and sucked vigorously for a few seconds before casting it aside. In a few moments he began to cry.

"Try sitting him up," Mrs. MacGregor suggested. "Maybe he doesn't like to be on his back." They experimented with various positions, and with each one Charlie cried louder, his face turning red and large tears squeezing out the corners of his eyes.

"Let me try," Mrs. MacGregor said. She put the baby over her shoulder and walked him back and forth across the room, murmuring in a low voice. The cries subsided to whimpers. "June, let's get that bottle. Could you warm it for me? Heat a pan of hot water on the burner and submerge the bottle in it for a few minutes. Then test the milk on the inside of your wrist. It should just be lukewarm on your skin."

June brought her the bottle and Mrs. MacGregor eased Charlie onto his back and put the nipple to his lips. He shook his head vigorously back and forth, pursing his mouth. She began to hum, walking him. Charlie quit crying and gazed up at her, his mouth slightly ajar. Mrs. MacGregor gently pushed the nipple between his lips, still humming. Without taking his eyes off her or blinking, Charlie began sucking. In five minutes he had finished the bottle. He let it fall from his mouth and smiled.

"I'm impressed," June said. "You certainly look experienced."

"It's funny how you don't forget some things. You take him now. My arms aren't as strong as they used to be."

Charlie welcomed June back with a smile, and began busily sucking and chewing on his fists. June played with him on the blanket for a while, and, at Mrs. MacGregor's suggestion, turned him over onto his stomach so he could practice crawling. He lay there squirming and lifting his head up, without going anywhere. When he got frustrated, June picked him up again, and was showing him the Christmas lights when Renata knocked. She had a sleek new haircut, which made her white neck look longer.

Charlie greeted her with enthusiastic razzing sounds when she picked him up. Back in his mother's arms he looked at June and Mrs. MacGregor, dividing beneficent smiles between them.

"How'd he do?"

"Just fine," Mrs. MacGregor said firmly. "You should leave him with a baby-sitter at least once a week. It's not healthy for you never to get away."

"You're right. I had completely forgotten what it was like to walk down the street without watching for ruts in the sidewalk that would catch on his stroller, or bending forward every two minutes to check on his hat. I actually just walked, looking in shop windows, crossing streets against the light, running up stairs. It was incredible. You get so you think the stroller is part of your body. Then, when you take a walk without it, you're suddenly just yourself again."

"Nice haircut," June said. She was thinking that maybe she should cut hers short like Renata's. It looked so clean and modern. June had kept her hair waist-length since she was fourteen.

"Thanks. That was heaven, too. You were so right, Eleanor. There's something about having someone else wash your hair that seems the height of luxury."

"When my children were small, I made sure I had my hair appointment and manicure once a week."

"Well, I really appreciate you two watching Charlie. I can tell he had a good time because he's so calm now." She turned to June. "Do you baby-sit a lot?"

"Not since high school. And not ever babies this young," June said.

"You seem very comfortable with him."

"She was excellent. Some people are naturally good with babies," Mrs. M. said.

"Well, I'm going to be looking for a regular sitter after the first of the year. Do you think you might be interested? I know Eleanor thinks the world of you. If we spent time together before I started the job, I think you'd be able to learn everything you need to know. One thing I found out when he was born is that nobody starts out an expert," Renata said, smiling.

"I go to school during the day," June said.

"I'm working nights at a downtown restaurant. I'll need a baby-sitter about thirty hours a week, but most of that will be after he goes to bed, so you could do homework while you're over. My shift is from five to midnight, Wednesday through Saturday."

June calculated fast. Her dance classes were first thing in the morning next semester, and the rest of her classes got out by two. Then she had Mrs. M. on Tuesdays and Fridays.

"I'm here until four-thirty on Fridays," June said. "What time do you have to leave for work?"

"Four-thirty, I'd say."

"That's perfect, June," Mrs. MacGregor said. "All you have to do is go right next door. You were telling me you were looking for an-other job. I'll be your baby consultant. But June has so much common sense, I doubt she'll ever need me," Mrs. MacGregor told Renata.

"Well—sure. I'd love to have the job," June said. It wasn't as if she needed to save her weekend nights for a boyfriend or anything.

"Great. Let's try it out, see how it goes," Renata said. "Do you think you could come over sometime next week and spend some more time with him? I'll show you all his routines." She turned to Mrs. MacGregor. "Why don't you join us when we're done, Eleanor, and I'll cook dinner."

June admired the way Renata could just say "Eleanor" instead of "Mrs. MacGregor." It made them seem woman-to-woman, as if age were an irrelevancy.

A week later the three of them were having dinner together at Re-nata's. She had made spaghetti and salad and served little individual bakery tarts for dessert.

"You were right about June having a knack for babies," Renata was telling Mrs. M. "Today he went off into the other room to play with her without even so much as a backward glance at me. And then tonight he let her bathe him and put him down for bed with a bottle. I was amazed."

"You're lucky. I remember having a nanny once that the children simply loathed. One day I pretended to go out just so I could go down to the cellar and put my ear to the furnace duct, trying to hear if she beat them when I was gone."

"And did she?" Renata asked.

"I don't think so. My plan didn't work as well as I hoped. I could hear every word they said when they were in the kitchen, but as soon as they moved to the playroom I only heard murmurs. But it didn't sound like she was being cruel. I think they just decided that she was repugnant for some reason—maybe she had foul breath, or a mole, who knows. Eventually I had to let her go because they made such a fuss about her. You'll see," Mrs. MacGregor said with a smile. "Your pleasant young man will find not-so-pleasant tactics for making his will known. They can be quite tyrannical, children."

June felt a little shy tonight. Mrs. M. and Renata found so much to talk about. Renata seemed to spark a liveliness in Mrs. MacGregor, this gossiping about feeding schedules and sleeping patterns, remedies for colic and cradle cap. June hadn't realized there was such a timelessness to the work of tending babies. She would have assumed that Mrs. M.'s experience would be somehow outdated next to Renata's. But it wasn't the case. As mothers, the two of them met across a divide of generations as casually as if it were a picket fence they shared between their yards. June knew they weren't trying to make her feel left out; but she did feel very much the spectator, the uninitiated. Yet it was cozy, listening to them.

Renata turned to her. "June, that nice guy at the desk, Owen, was telling me you're going to New York soon."

June was embarrassed. Renata's eyebrows were lifted in question. Mrs. MacGregor was looking at her closely. "Oh, no, not soon," she stammered. "I just mentioned that if I ever really wanted to be a dancer, New York would be the place to do it." Now she was lying about her lie.

"I didn't realize that you were a dancer," Renata said.

"Well, you know, I'd like to be. I've studied for years. And New York is where all the important dance companies are."

"You wouldn't quit school, would you, June?" Mrs. MacGregor asked.

"No, not if I didn't have anything definite lined up. But I could always go down this summer and check things out, and then come back to school in the fall." She was making it up as she went along, but it sounded good.

"That's probably what Owen was referring to. He made it sound like you were leaving next week," Renata said.

"I guess maybe I left him with that impression," June said. "He was trying to get me to go skiing with him, and I didn't really want to."

"He seems like a nice young man," Mrs. MacGregor observed.

"But you must admit, Eleanor," Renata said, "he's not exactly June's type. Too, too . . ."

"Nerdy," June said.

Renata laughed. "Exactly. We want someone a bit more fun for June."

"There's nothing wrong with a steady, reliable fellow. Fun wears out," Mrs. MacGregor warned.

"Tell us about your husband, Eleanor," Renata urged, pouring them more wine. "Was he steady and reliable, or was he fun?"

Mrs. MacGregor frowned slightly and sat back in her chair. June thought Renata had overstepped. You didn't barge into Mrs. M.'s personal life unless you were invited. To her surprise, Mrs. Mac-Gregor took a sip of wine and reflected.

"He was steady and reliable, *and* fun," she pronounced. "He knew how to have a good time." She seemed on the verge of continuing, then took another sip of wine and stopped. She looked at June. "It *is* important that they know how to make you laugh," she said.

"But it's also important that there's more to them than that," Renata said, a sudden emphasis behind her words. "Listen to Eleanor, June, not me."

June and Mrs. MacGregor looked at her, waiting for her to elaborate. But Renata just stood and began clearing the table. June rose to help her.

"Well, ladies, should I open another bottle of wine?" Renata asked, holding up the empty bottle.

"Goodness, no," Mrs. MacGregor said. "I shouldn't be drinking at my age, and I don't think June shouldn't be drinking at *her* age."

"And I shouldn't be drinking at any age," Renata said.

June had begun to notice that Renata never fully explained herself. In fact, all three of them seemed to have little doors that they began to open to each other, but only partially. Just when you started to see around the door to what was inside, it closed. Even so, it was a wonderful evening. Sitting in Renata's kitchen with the two of them made June feel part of something. On the way back to her apartment, June found herself humming the song Renata had taught her as they did the dishes, something about three Irish maids, and their hard Irish luck.

© CLARK QUIN

SUZANNE MATSON was born in Portland, Oregon, and studied at Portland State University and the University of Washington in Seattle. She is the author of two volumes of poetry, *Sea Level* and *Durable Goods*. Her poems and essays have appeared in *American Poetry Review*, *Harvard Review*, and *The New York Times Magazine*. She teaches at Boston College and lives in Newton, Massachusetts, with her husband and two young sons.

IN DARK WATER

Mermer Blakeslee

Dear BRC Reader,

It's a genuine pleasure to introduce you to a mesmerizing novel we're publishing in paperback in May: *In Dark Water* by Mermer Blakeslee. If you like the work of Jane Hamilton, Jacquelyn Mitchard or Connie May Fowler, I think you'll be moved by this powerful work. In fact, Connie May Fowler herself called the book, "a triumph of the spirit . . . a novel of uncommon grace and soaring beauty."

As an editor, I'm always looking for novels that illuminate some aspect of our shared experience, that remind us of our roots. This is a book that will make you remember all the mystery, confusion, and joy of childhood. It's the story of a family dealing with unthinkable tragedy, but discovering the common ground that pulls them back together.

Mermer is a passionate writer who unearths the profundity inherent in seemingly ordinary people and things. I hope you'll be as taken with her book as I am.

Peter K. Borland
Executive Editor

Fat

I was the youngest person and the littlest by a lot that ever got to work at the Petersons' farm. I had to do four stalls a day and that meant I could ride for a whole hour. But usually I did Twinkle's stall, too, and sometimes even Nighty's, so I was Mrs. Peterson's favorite. I didn't even have to call her Mrs. Peterson after a while 'cause no other students did, and even though they were all adults, it didn't matter I was a kid, I could call her Mary. And even her husband, I called him Buddy.

I went every day after school. I rode on Mr. Holcomb's bus and most days I could get all my homework done by the time he left me off at the farm. Then Dad would pick me up after he finished work, which was getting later and later, so I started to eat supper more and more at the farm 'cause they always ate early, around five, and then Mary would teach her evening lessons now that it was staying light longer. "To make ends meet," she said. At first they pulled up an extra chair for me but then they stopped putting it back against the wall, it was my seat and even if I wasn't there a few days, when I came back, the chair was still at the table. Mary's mother did all the cooking and she always cooked too much. "Finish it," she'd say. "Finish it, I wanna get rid of it." But still she'd make more the next day and too much again.

Mary would be teaching already when I got off the bus but she'd leave the horse I was supposed to ride in the barn for me to lead out and join the lesson in the big ring. Then, after supper, I'd stand by the gate and watch and sometimes she'd yell for me to pick up a crop or fix a cavalletti. I liked most the days no one was scheduled. Then I'd help her groom the horses. "There!" she'd say whenever we finished one and she was unclipping the cross-tie. "Now I just have to throw a quick brush on him in the morning." That made it a lot easier for her 'cause she had to get them all ready and tacked up before eight. Some days it was raining hard and I wouldn't get to ride but it didn't matter, it was better than going home. And it got better and better the more work I knew how to do. "You are such a help to me," Mary would say about two or three times a day and she meant it, too, 'cause even though I was little, I could carry a five-gallon bucket full of water from the pump to the farthest stall where Nicky was. Even Buddy, who didn't ever say much, said, "Would you believe that?"

I never told Mary that I didn't want to go home but I think she guessed. And one time she even said, "If you ever need to stay here for any reason, you know you can," but then the truck from Five Oak Farm pulled up so she didn't say anything more.

Dad would pick me up most nights around seven or seven-thirty but sometimes he'd call and wouldn't come till nine and then I'd be there to help her hay in the horses and water them for the night. I loved that the best. And when Mary came in from the barn and Buddy came in, too, from the garage, which was full of people's furniture he was fixing, whenever they got back in, they'd sit down and eat a bowl of ice cream. And sometimes Dad was late enough so I got one, too.

It was one of the nights my dad came late that I found out about Bogey. He got cut to only three quarters instead of a whole can of feed. When I asked why, Mary said, "Well . . ." and kept on scooping the grain up so I knew not to ask again. But still I couldn't help myself. "Why doesn't he get a full can anymore?"

"Well, Eudora . . ." She paused a long time but I waited, even after she handed me the full can and said, "Nicky," even then I waited and she said, "There's a hard side to this business."

I nodded and kept waiting.

"Well, you see, Eudora, he's not going to ever be sold." I took the feed to Nicky's stall, and came back to trade her the empty can for the two full ones she had ready for me. "Proud. Thaddeus."

When I came back to trade cans, she asked, "Understand? Here. Baron. Showtime. Understand, Eudora?" I almost nodded. I knew this was one of those times I was just supposed to nod, not push. "She pushes," is what *she* had just said to Dad about me. And Mrs. Klepp, too, had said to the principal, "That girl never knows when to stop." But I didn't nod, it was too fast, I took the cans and I shook my head, no, I didn't understand, and then I turned away quick to continue the feeding.

"I can't afford to keep him going," she said but her voice was deep into the feed bin. It was Monday night and Dean's Mills delivered a new load every Tuesday so only her legs showed each time she scraped a can of feed up. Her voice sounded eerie from in there. When she came back out, she handed me the last two cans. "Twinkle. Son. And that's it for tonight, I'll get Nighty's and Chesty's." They got a tablespoon of vegetable oil and a scoop of vitamins in theirs.

But I didn't turn away 'cause Mary was looking at me. "We're going to put Bogey down." She watched me hear it.

"But—" I started.

She shook her head. "He's too old to sell. Except to the glue factory. And I'd *never* do that."

I knew not to ask any more questions. I watched her feed her two horses that only she rode. She wouldn't use them for lessons.

She was looking at me again as she walked back with the empty cans to throw into the feed bin before she put a clip on it so no raccoons could get in. "It's the hard part, Eudora. I can't afford it and I can't afford to let him go fat into the grave."

Fat into the grave. I couldn't get it out of my head. Every day after that, when I ran into the barn, I looked first to see if he was still there. And even before I looked to see who was saddled for me to ride, I'd go into his stall and check if I could feel his ribs. His coat was still shiny even though it was heavier now than the others. I rubbed my hands back and forth over his side. I couldn't feel any bone, and I'd think, *Fat into the grave. Going fat into the grave.*

In school, it went around and around in my brain on its own, *fat into the grave.* Every time I wasn't thinking or doing work, if I was just writing down our homework, I could hear it going on in the background, *fat into the grave.*

Each day on the bus I thought, *Maybe today, maybe I'll walk into the barn and he'll be gone. Disappeared.* I wanted to see it. But I never thought, *Ask, just ask.* Till it popped into my brain out in the hall.

I ended up in the hall 'cause I hated Mrs. Klepp. So when she asked me why I didn't finish my homework, nothing came into my

brain except what I said. " 'Cause the bus ride wasn't long enough."
And when she asked, "What?" to give me a second chance, I didn't
make up something else, I said the same thing over again and it came
onto my face, I felt it come, the smile.

That was it. She knew I hated her then and that was better, I
thought, than just being bad. She stood up from her desk and said,
"Okay, Miss Buell." She called me Miss Buell when she was really
mad. "Okay. Okay." She kept saying, "Okay. Okay," as she walked
straight to my desk. "Get up! Come on! Up! Out of your chair." I took
my notebook and pencil with me. And then she picked the whole
desk with the chair hooked to it off the floor. I could hear all the books
slide down inside. I thought she was going to take it to the back corner where I sat for a week at the beginning of the year, but instead,
she wheeled around with it and walked to the front of the room.
Some of my pencils fell out. Mary Beth leaned over to grab one and
then she got up to get the rest from the floor. She gave them to Peggy,
who sat right in front of me. I knew Peggy was waiting for me to look
at her. Mary Beth and Peggy were both looking, waiting in case
I needed to look back at them, but I didn't, I watched Mrs. Klepp
instead. I watched her walk out the door. And then I stood there a
moment, even after Peggy handed me my pencils and whispered,
"Witch," I stood there in the empty spot where my desk used to be.

I heard my desk and chair slam down in the hall just outside the
door. "There!" Mrs. Klepp said, just like Mary finishing a horse. Mrs.
Klepp walked back in the room so I looked down. I didn't want her to
catch my eyes. I made it out the door without her catching my eyes.
"Till the end of the year," she said but that was only a little over a
month.

It was darker out in the hall. I started the copying. She always
makes anyone who's bad copy a hundred times the quote she writes
on the board each day. I always write all the numbers down the side
of the page first. Today's was " 'It is better to know some of the questions than all of the answers.' James Thurber." You had to write the
man's name each time.

I was right next to the wall. The yellow tiles ended above my head,
and I felt where they curved into the regular wall, which was always
shiny white. Walking to music or gym, I'd always be next to the wall
so I could walk with my hand cupped over that curve. But what I
wanted now was the cold. I pressed my whole side flat against the
tiles so I could feel the cold seep into my arm.

It didn't last long. I only got to number 36 and my arm had already turned the tiles warm. I wanted more cold. I pressed my cheek against another tile farther up. I waited till the cold spread completely over my face. I liked it out here. I could think. The cold helped me think. I knew 'cause it was right then it came to me to *ask* Mary, Mrs. Peterson, what I had been wanting but never thought to ask for. I could just ask. It seemed so simple. Cold always made things simple.

I was afraid of one thing, though. What if Mary asked back, "Why?" I didn't know. I only knew I had to see him fall, go into the hole. Anything, I'd watch anything, even if there was blood, as long as he didn't just disappear.

I waited till after five when all the other riding students had driven away and we were about to go in to eat supper. There were no lessons scheduled for the night.

"Mary?" I had practiced so many times the exact question but still my mouth felt dry. I closed my eyes.

"What is it?" she asked. "What?"

"Can I see you put Bogey down?" *There!* I thought. *I did it, it's over.*

She was quiet for so long I thought maybe she hadn't heard, except she stopped walking. She was standing at the gate that separates the barnyard from the lawn. I just waited. I looked at the ground and waited.

"I don't know," she finally said. "I don't know. Why?" I shook my head. I couldn't look up. "Why, dear? Why do you want to?" but I kept shaking my head. I could feel tears behind my eyes so now I definitely couldn't look up. If she saw me cry just asking, she'd never let me watch a horse get killed. I kept shaking my head. She knelt down and held my arms. "Eudora?"

"I don't know," I said, and all my hope left that she'd say yes. "I just don't want to see him gone, have him gone without . . . without seeing it."

She stood back up but she was still touching the top of my shoulder. "Okay," she said. I couldn't really believe it but then she said, "Next Saturday he's coming, pretty early. You should be here by nine."

I let out a big breath. I had only thought about asking. I had practiced in my brain only the asking part. I never thought about after, about right now, about her actually saying yes, that I could see it. I thought for a second I was going to get sick but I swallowed it back. It was only for a second.

Saturday, I knew the date, May 26, 'cause it was my birthday. But I didn't tell Mary that. I didn't want her to know. Dad had already explained to me out in the garage why I couldn't have a party. The doctor had said no, it would be too much for her. But I knew it anyway, I knew it as soon as he said, "Your birthday is coming up. How old are you gonna be?" I knew right then they had talked to the doctor. He hugged me when he said, "I'm sorry about it, Eudora, I'm sorry. Really, I am, I'm sorry." He always repeated everything but I didn't mind. It made the hug last longer.

On the way home in the car that night, I felt lucky. It was all perfect. I could ask Dad to drive me to the Petersons' on my birthday, that Mrs. Peterson had said it was okay even though it was Saturday. And he'd say, "Yes, of course." He'd never think to ask if I was riding or not.

She came into my room that morning and kissed my forehead, counting each kiss, "One year, two years, three years . . ." all the way up to eleven. "Eleven years old!" And then she sat down beside me. "Happy birthday." I curled up and smiled under the blankets, but not for what she thought. I was sneaking my birthday. I felt almost bad but not, not really. It was like a real birthday that was going to happen inside the regular birthday.

When Dad left me off, Buddy had already dug the hole. It was in the field with the old apple trees back of the barn. There was a big pile of dirt beside his backhoe and beside that, the hole. I looked in. It was so much bigger than a horse.

When Hogan's truck came, Mary told me to stand back with Buddy. Mary led Bogey out beside the hole and fed him a scoop of grain in the black bucket Buddy had brought out before. He still didn't have any ribs showing. Bogey was eating with his head down when Mary said, "Okay," and the man came out from behind the truck and laid the gun right between his eyes and shot. Bogey fell sideways. I saw a little grain drop from his lips and then he was gone, he was in the hole. I heard him land. "There!" Mary said, but then she turned away. She brushed her hair back over her head and let out a big sigh. "Done."

Buddy and I walked up. The hole seemed smaller now. Bogey's neck was bent to its shape and his face was turned up toward us. His mouth was open, so I could see what was left of his teeth, worn down to almost nothing. There were little clumps of grain all over them and over his lips, too. "Died eating," Buddy said. "You could go worse." I didn't know what I felt, if I felt anything, but I moved my shoulders and arms around like something big had just happened. I moved them to find out: Were they different now? Was everything different? But there was no blood on his face, not even a drop. I couldn't even see the hole in his head. Everything had happened inside.

Buddy said, later, it's the kind of bullet they use, it's small and it explodes in their brain and kills them instantly. "More humane than a needle," he said. "T.D., he needed three shots before he fell." That was the last time they used the vet. "Costs more, too," he said, "by the time you get him out here."

Mary asked if I wanted to go inside the house. She was going to make some tea but I didn't go in with her. Instead, I watched Buddy on the backhoe scoop up all the dirt and dump it into the hole. I watched until the pile was gone and Buddy was using the loader to scrape the ground flat.

Graveyards are never flat. The ground sinks in wherever the graves are. In front of every stone, you see a hollow almost the shape of the coffin. I didn't want to ever go back to David's grave 'cause I didn't want to see the hollow. I didn't know how long that would take but I didn't care. I never wanted to see it, ever. They went every Sunday but I stayed in the car. I wouldn't get out. I looked away from them, out the window on the opposite side. I didn't mind seeing the ripples in the ground on that side and if I squinted they even seemed like a sea of water, green water like where Uncle Peter lives in Maine, with lots of white sails sticking up.

When Buddy turned off the motor, I walked into the house. "Well, now you've seen it," Mary said. I nodded. "Still want horses?" I nodded again. "They all go, one way or another."

"Yeah," I said. I felt eleven, and eleven seemed so much older than ten, much more than a year, just the sound of it, *eleven*.

"Have a cup of tea with me," she said. I had never had one before. She showed me how to press out the tea bag with the spoon. "So you get more tea," she explained. I put lots of milk and two teaspoons of sugar in it. I cupped my hands around it while I sipped at it. It was just the right hot and just the right sweet. I didn't want Dad to come ever.

© ERO STUBBLEFIELD

MERMER BLAKESLEE is also the author of the novel *Same Blood*. In 1998, she received a fiction fellowship from The New York Foundation for the Arts. Ms. Blakeslee lives with her husband and son in New York's Catskill Mountains.

BLACK GLASS

Karen Joy Fowler

Dear BRC Reader,

Karen Joy Fowler is one of my favorite writers, one whose work I enjoy as a reader, as well as a publisher. I first came across her work when visiting Denver, Colorado. There, I was browsing through the Tattered Cover Bookstore for some pleasure reading, and *The Sweetheart Season* was recommended to me. I completely devoured it on the plane ride home; I was so taken with the book that I immediately contacted Henry Holt, the hardcover publisher, for the reprint rights. And I am not alone in my praise for Karen Joy Fowler: the novels *The Sweetheart Season* and *Sarah Canary* have both been named *New York Times* Notable Books. Her gifts of narrative and character make her texts resonate with a mythic and wondrous power. The following is a short fiction from *Black Glass*—a small taste of this talented author's succulent prose.

Judith Curr
Senior Vice-President and Publisher

There is no evidence that Elizabeth ever blamed her father for killing her mother. Of course, she would hardly have remembered her mother. At three months, Elizabeth had been moved into her own household with her own servants; her parents became visitors rather than caretakers. At three years, the whole affair was history—her mother's head on Tower Green, her father's remarriage eleven days later. Because the charge was adultery and, in one case, incest, her own parentage might easily have come into question. But there has never been any doubt as to who her father was. "The lion's cub," she called herself, her father's daughter, and from him she got her red hair, her white skin, her dancing, her gaiety, her predilection for having relatives beheaded, and her sex.

Her sex was the problem, of course. Her mother's luck at cards had been bad all summer. But the stars were good, the child rode low in the belly, and the pope, they had agreed, was powerless. They were expecting a boy.

After the birth, the jousts and tournaments had to be canceled. The musicians were sent away, except for a single piper, frolicsome but thin. Her mother, spent and sick from childbirth, felt the cold breath of disaster on her neck.

Her father put the best face on it. Wasn't she healthy? Full weight and lusty? A prince would surely follow. A poor woman gave the princess a rosemary bush hung all with gold spangles. "Isn't that nice?" her mother's ladies said brightly, as if it weren't just a scented branch with glitter.

Elizabeth had always loved her father. She watched sometimes when he held court. She saw the deference he commanded. She saw how careful he was. He could not allow himself to be undone with passion or with pity. The law was the law, he told the women who came before him. A woman's wages belonged to her husband. He could mortgage her property if he liked, forfeit it to creditors. That his children were hungry made no difference. The law acknowledged the defect of her sex. Her father could not do less.

He would show the women these laws in his books. He would show Elizabeth. She would make a little mark with her fingernail in the margin beside them. Some night when he was asleep, some night when she had more courage than she had ever had before, she would slip into the library and cut the laws she had marked out of the books. Then the women would stop weeping and her father would be able to do as he liked.

Her father read to her *The Taming of the Shrew*. He never seemed to see that she hated Petruchio with a passion a grown woman might have reserved for an actual man. "You should have been a boy," he told her, when she brought home the prize in Greek, ahead of all the boys in her class.

Her older brother died when she was a small girl. Never again was she able to bear the sound of a tolling bell. She went with her father to the graveyard, day after day. He threw himself on the grave, arms outstretched. At home, he held her in his arms and wept onto her sleeve, into her soft brown hair. "My daughter," he said. His arms tightened. "If only you had been a boy."

She tried to become a boy. She rode horseback, learned Latin. She remained a girl. She sewed. She led the Presbyterian Girls' Club. The club baked and stitched to earn the money to put a deserving young man through seminary. When he graduated, they went as a group to see him preach his first sermon. They sat in the front. He stood up in the clothes they had made for him. "There is a lesson we have for today," he said from the pulpit. "First Timothy, chapter two, verse twelve: 'I suffer not a woman to teach, nor to usurp authority over the man, but be in silence.' "

Elizabeth rose. She walked down the long aisle of the church and out into the street. The sun was so fiery it blinded her for a moment. She stood at the top of the steps, waiting until she could see them. The door behind her opened. It opened again and again. The Presbyterian Girls' Club had all come with her.

She had, they said, a pride like summer. She rode horseback, learned Latin and also Greek, which her father had never studied. One winter day she sat with all her ladies in the park, under an oak, under a canopy, stitching with her long, beautiful, white fingers. If the other ladies were cold, if they wished to be inside, they didn't say so. They sat and sewed together, and one of them sang aloud and the snowflakes flew about the tent like moths. Perhaps Elizabeth was herself cold and wouldn't admit it, or perhaps, even thin as she was, she was not cold and this would be an even greater feat. There was no way to know which was true.

Perhaps Elizabeth was merely teasing. Her fingers rose and dipped quickly over the cloth. From time to time, she joined her merry voice to the singer's. She had a strong animal aura, a force. Her spirits were always lively. John Knox denounced her in church for her fiddling and flinging. She and her sister both, he said, were incurably addicted to joyosity.

Her half brother had never been lusty. When he died, some years after her father, long after his own mother, hail the color of fire fell in the city, thunder rolled low and continuous through the air. This was a terrible time. It was her time.

Her father opposed her marriage. It was not marriage itself he opposed; no, he had hoped for that. It was the man. A dangerous radical. An abolitionist. A man who would never earn money. A man who could then take her money. Hadn't she sat in his court and seen this often enough with her very own eyes?.

For a while she was persuaded. When she was strong enough, she rebelled. She insisted that the word *obey* be stricken from the ceremony. Nor would she change her name. "There is a great deal in a name," she wrote her girlfriend. "It often signifies much and may involve a great principle. This custom is founded on the principle that white men are lords of all. I cannot acknowledge this principle as just; therefore I cannot bear the name of another." She meant her first name by this. She meant Elizabeth.

Her family's power and position went back to the days when Charles I sat on the English throne. Her father was astonishingly wealthy, spectacularly thrifty. He wasted no money on electricity, bathrooms, or telephones. He made small, short-lived exceptions for his youngest daughter. She bought a dress; she took a trip abroad. She was dreadfully spoiled, they said later.

But spinsters are generally thought to be entitled to compensatory trips abroad, and she had reached the age where marriage was unlikely. Once men had come to court her in the cramped parlor. They faltered under the grim gaze of her father. There is no clear evidence that she ever blamed him for this, although there is, of course, the unclear evidence.

She did not get on with her stepmother. "I do not call her mother," she said. She herself was exactly the kind of woman her father esteemed—quiet, reserved, respectful. Lustless and listless. She got from him her wide beautiful eyes, her sky-colored eyes, her chestnut hair.

When Elizabeth was one year old, her father displayed her, quite naked, to the French ambassadors. They liked what they saw. Negotiations began to betroth her to the Duke of Angoulême, negotiations that foundered later for financial reasons.

She was planning to address the legislature. Her father read it in the paper. He called her into the library and sat with her before the fire. The blue and orange flames wrapped around the logs, whispering into smoke. "I beg you not to do this," he said. "I beg you not to disgrace me in my old age. I'll give you the house in Seneca Falls."

She had been asking for the house for years. "No," Elizabeth said.

"Then I'll disinherit you entirely."

"If you must."

"Let me hear this speech."

As he listened his eyes filled with tears. "Surely, you have had a comfortable and happy life," he cried out. "Everything you could have wanted has been supplied. How can someone so tenderly brought up feel such things? Where did you learn such bitterness?"

"I learnt it here," she told him. "Here, when I was a child, listening to the women who brought you their injustices." Her own eyes, fixed on his unhappy face, spilled over. "Myself, I am happy," she told him. "I have everything. You've always loved me. I know this."

He waited a long time in silence. "You've made your point clear," he said finally. "But I think I can find you even more cruel laws than those you've quoted." Together they reworked the speech. On toward morning, they kissed each other and retired to their bedrooms. She delivered her words to the legislature. "You are your father's daughter," the senators told her afterward, gracious if unconvinced. "Today, your father would be proud."

"Your work is a continual humiliation to me," he said. "To me, who's had the respect of my colleagues and my country all my life.

You have seven children. Take care of them." The next time she spoke publicly he made good on his threats and removed her from his will.

"Thank God for a girl," her mother said when Elizabeth was born. She fell into an exhausted sleep. When she awoke she looked more closely. The baby's arms and shoulders were thinly dusted with dark hair. She held her eyes tightly shut, and when her mother forced them open, she could find no irises. The doctor was not alarmed. The hair was hypertrichosis, he said. It would disappear. Her eyes were fine. Her father said that she was beautiful.

It took Elizabeth ten days to open her eyes on her own. At the moment she did, it was her mother who was gazing straight into them. They were already violet.

When she was three years old they attended the silver jubilee for George V. She wore a Parisian dress of organdie. Her father tried to point out the royal ladies. "Look at the King's horse!" Elizabeth said instead. The first movie she was ever taken to see was *The Little Princess* with Shirley Temple.

Her father had carried her in his arms. He dressed all in joyous yellow. He held her up for the courtiers to see. When he finally had a son, he rather lost interest. He wrote his will to clarify the order of succession. At this point, he felt no need to legitimize his daughters, although he did recognize their place in line for the throne. He left Elizabeth an annual income of three thousand pounds. And if she ever married without sanction, the will stated, she was to be removed from the line of succession, "as though the said Lady Elizabeth were then dead."

She never married. Like Penelope, she maintained power by promising to marry first this and then that man; she turned her miserable sex to her advantage. She made an infamous number of these promises. No other woman in history has begun so many engagements and died a maid. "The Queen did fish for men's souls and had so sweet a bait that no one could escape from her network," they said at court. She had a strong animal aura.

A muskiness. When she got married for the first time her father gave her away. She was only seventeen years old and famously beautiful, the last brunette in a world of blondes. Her father was a guest at her third wedding. "This time I hope her dreams come true," he told the reporters. "I wish her the happiness she so deserves." He was a guest at her fifth wedding, as well.

Her parents had separated briefly when she was fourteen years old. Her mother, to whom she had always been closer, had an affair with someone on the set; her father took her brother and went home to his parents. Elizabeth may have said that his moving out was no special loss. She has been quoted as having said this.

She never married. She married seven different men. She married once and had seven children. She never married. The rack was in constant use during the latter half of her reign. Unexplained illnesses plagued her. It was the hottest day of the year, a dizzying heat. She went into the barn for Swansea pears. Inexplicably the loft was cooler than the house. She said she stayed there half an hour in the slatted light, the half coolness. Her father napped inside the house.

"I perceive you think of our father's death with a calm mind," her half brother, the new king, noted.

"It was a pleasant family to be in?" the Irish maid was asked. Her name was Bridget, but she was called Maggie by the girls, because they had once had another Irish maid they were fond of and she'd had that name.

"I don't know how the family was. I got along all right."

"You never saw anything out of the way?"

"No, sir."

"You never saw any conflict in the family?"

"No, sir."

"Never saw the least—any quarreling or anything of that kind?"

"No, sir."

The half hour between her father settling down for his nap and the discovery of murder may well be the most closely examined half hour in criminal history. The record is quite specific as to the times. When Bridget left the house, she looked at the clock. As she ran, she heard the city hall bell toll. Only eight minutes are unaccounted for.

After the acquittal she changed her name to Lizbeth. "There is one thing that hurts me very much," she told the papers. "They say I don't show any grief. They say I don't cry. They should see me when I am alone."

Her father died a brutal, furious, famous death. Her father died quietly of a stroke before her sixth wedding. After her father died, she discovered he had reinserted her into his will. She had never doubted that he loved her. She inherited his great fortune, along with her sister. She found a sort of gaiety she'd never had before.

She became a devotee of the stage, often inviting whole casts home for parties, food, and dancing. Her sister was horrified; despite the acquittal they had become a local grotesquerie. The only seemly response was silence, her sister told Lizbeth, who responded to this damp admonition with another party.

The sound of a pipe and tabor floated through the palace. Lord Semphill went looking for the source of the music. He found the queen dancing with Lady Warwick. When she had become queen, she had taken a motto. SEMPER EADEM, it was. ALWAYS THE SAME. This motto had first belonged to her mother.

She noticed Lord Semphill watching her through the drapes. "Your father loved to dance," he said awkwardly, for he had always been told this. He was embarrassed to be caught spying on her.

"Won't you come and dance with us?" she asked. She was laughing at him. Why not laugh? She had survived everything and everyone. She held out her arms. Lord Semphill was suddenly deeply moved to see the queen—at her age!—bending and leaping into the air like the flame on a candle, twirling this way and then that, like the tongue in a lively bell.

KAREN JOY FOWLER is the author of two novels, *Sarah Canary* and *The Sweetheart Season*—both *New York Times* Notable Books—and one story collection, *Artificial Things*. She lives in Davis, California.

WHAT WE KEEP

Elizabeth Berg

Dear BRC Reader,

If you haven't discovered Elizabeth Berg, you don't know what you're missing. Her books speak to the heart and to the imagination. To read Elizabeth Berg is to be moved and forever changed by characters that are so real and vivid, they will stay with you long after you've finished the last page.

What We Keep is no exception. In this rich and deeply satisfying story, a reunion between two sisters and their mother reveals how the secrets and complexities of the past have shaped the lives of the women in a family. It is a story that speaks to the heart of what matters to us most, with emotional honesty and a true understanding of people and relationships.

Elizabeth Berg writes books you will want to share with your best friends, your sister, your mother, your daughter. And they are books you will re-read, and enjoy just as much as the first time. So experience Elizabeth Berg for yourself—it's like discovering a new friend you feel you've known your whole life.

Shauna Summers
Senior Editor

Outside the airplane window the clouds are thick and rippled, un-broken as acres of land. They are suffused with peach-colored, early morning sun, gilded at the edges. Across the aisle, a man is taking a picture of them. Even the pilot couldn't keep still—"Folks," he just said, "we've got quite a sunrise out there. Might want to have a look." I like it when pilots make such comments. It lets me know they're awake.

Whenever I see a sight like these clouds, I think maybe everyone is wrong; maybe you *can* walk on air. Maybe we should just try. Every-thing could have changed without our noticing. Laws of physics, I mean. Why not? I want it to be true that such miracles occur. I want to stop the plane, put the kickstand down, and have us all file out there, shrugging airline claustrophobia off our shoulders. I want us to be able to breathe easily this high up, to walk on clouds as if we were an-gels, to point out our houses to each other way, way, way down there; and there; and there. How proud we would suddenly feel about where we live, how tender toward everything that's ours—our Mix-masters, resting on kitchen counters; our children, wearing the socks we bought them and going about children's business; our mail lying on our desks; our gardens, tilled and expectant. It seems to me it would just come with the perspective, this rich appreciation.

I lean my forehead against the glass, sigh. I am forty-seven years old and these longings come to me with the same seriousness and fre-quency that they did when I was a child.

"Long trip, huh?" the woman next to me asks.

"Oh," I say. "Yes. Although . . . Well, I sighed because I wish I could get out. You know? Get out there and walk around."

She looks past me, through the window. "Pretty," she says. And then, "Of course, you'd die."

"Oh, well. What's not dangerous?"

"Beats me," the woman says. "Not food. Not water. Not air, not sex. You can't do *anything*. Well, maybe put your name on the list for Biosphere." We smile, ruefully. She's pretty, a young blond business-woman wearing a stylish navy-blue suit, gold jewelry, soft-looking leather heels now slipped off her feet. At first, she busied herself with paperwork. Now she's bored and wants to talk. Fine with me. I'm bored, too.

"Do you ever think that this is the end of the world?" I ask. "I mean, don't get me wrong—"

"Oh, I know what you mean," she says. "I do think about that. Dy-ing planets, how . . . unspecial we are, really. Just the most current thing in the line since paramecia."

The flight attendant stops her cart beside us, asks if we'd like a drink. This seems petty, considering the content of our conversation. Still, I request orange juice; the woman beside me says she'd like a scotch.

"You know what?" I tell the flight attendant. "I think I'll have a scotch, too." I have always wondered who in the world would want a cocktail on an early morning flight. Now I know: people with a load on their minds that they would like very much to lighten.

After my seatmate and I have pulled down our trays and set up our impromptu bar, I say, "I don't even like scotch."

"Me neither." She shrugs, takes a sip, grimaces. "But I really hate flying. Sometimes this helps."

I smile, extend my hand. "I'm Ginny Young."

"Martha Hamilton."

"You live in California?"

"Yeah. San Francisco. You?"

"I live in Boston. I'm going to visit my mother. She lives in Mill Valley."

"Nice. How long since you've seen her?"

I do some math, then answer, "Thirty-five years."

Martha turns toward me, stares. I know her scotch is pooled in her mouth.

I shrug. "I don't like my mother. I'm not ashamed to say that. She's not a good person. She did some things . . . Well, she's not a good person." Whenever people I've met tell their mother horror stories, I save mine for last. It's the best, because it's the worst.

"So . . . why are you going to see her?"

"It was my sister's idea. She thinks she's sick. Not my mother— her."

"Is she?"

"Don't know. She's waiting for some test results. But she wanted to go and see our mother. Just . . . in case. You know. Unfinished business that she feels she needs to attend to."

Martha breathes out. "Jesus. I'm sorry."

"Well."

She touches my arm. "Are you all right?"

"Me? Yes! It's . . . this is old. It's so old. I didn't intend ever to see my mother again, and I was perfectly comfortable with that. I won't see her after this visit; I know that. I'm just doing this for my sister. Even though I don't really think she's sick. She can't be."

Martha nods, cracks an ice cube with her teeth, then looks at me, one eyebrow raised.

"Right," I say. "I know."

"I'll tell you something," Martha says. "I was in a cemetery last week, walking my dog. You're not supposed to walk your dog there, so when I heard someone coming, I hid behind this big marker. I saw a woman stop just a few graves away. She knelt down and started talking out loud. She was apparently talking about one of her kids who was giving her a really a hard time, and then she said, 'I didn't do that to you, Ma, did I? Did I?' And then she lay down and just started crying. She cried so *hard*! It was one of those things where the grief is so raw, you can't help yourself—you start crying, too. And when I started crying, my dog started barking. The woman looked up and saw me, of course. She got all embarrassed—jumped up and wiped her face, started straightening her clothes and rummaging around in her purse for something or other. And I felt terrible. It was terrible to have a dog there, those rules are absolutely right. I apologized, but I still felt like a jerk.

"All the way home, I wondered what that woman was crying about, what she had remembered. I wondered if other daughters talk to their mothers when they visit their graves, whether if, when my mother dies, I will. Seems like a good party question, doesn't it?— What would you say at your mother's grave? Well, maybe not a *party* question. But an interesting one. At least you'll have the chance to speak to her in person."

"Right," I say, although what I'm thinking is, there's nothing I want to tell my mother. I'm only going for Sharla. I love my sister; I'm finished with my mother, have been for a long time. Not for nothing did I sit in therapists' offices going through a forest's worth of Kleenex.

"Where does your sister live?" Martha asks.

"Texas. San Antonio. She'll be at the airport waiting; her flight gets in twenty minutes before mine."

"Has *she* seen your mother in all this time?"

"No."

"Wow. This will be some meeting."

"I know," I say, and drain what's left of the scotch. Then I squeeze the plastic glass to see how far I can bend it. Not far: it cracks in my hand. I put it in the throw-up bag, fold the top over, place it neatly in the center of my tray table. I don't want to talk anymore. I lean back, look out the window. I have my reasons, I tell myself—and Martha, too, in case she's picking up on my thoughts—she's from California, after all; they do stuff like that. But I do have my reasons. I absolutely do.

"Miss?" the flight attendant asks. "Breakfast?" I startle, then smile and nod yes to the fat slices of French toast she is offering me. I am probably the only one in the world who likes airline food. I appreciate the inventive garnishes, the only-for-you serving sizes. I like the taste of the salad dressings. When the entrée is something like pizza, I think, well, isn't that the cutest thing. Naturally, I don't admit this to anyone.

Martha has opted for the cheese omelet, and when I watch her cut it neatly in half, I wish I'd gotten one too. She shrugs after her first bite, the physical equivalent of "Yuck." I smile, shrug back, pour the thick artificial maple syrup over my French toast. It looks delicious.

"I saw a row of three across open back there," Martha says, after she's eaten most of her breakfast. "I think I'll go on back and stretch out for a while."

"Okay."

"Unless you were thinking of that, too. In that case, we could flip for it."

"No, this is fine," I say. "I'll have more room, too. Anyway, I'm not going to sleep."

"Really? Any plane trip over an hour, I have to sleep. Otherwise I get stir-crazy. Once I brought letters to read on an airplane. You know, the kind of thing you keep, thinking sometime you'd really like to read them again, but then you never do. I brought along this huge stack of letters from old boyfriends. I took them out and read them all. They passed the time all right, but it was so embarrassing— they made me cry. I'll never do that again! Better to go to sleep and embarrass yourself by drooling." She stands, opens the overhead bin and pulls down a pillow and a blanket, heads down the aisle.

I know what Martha means about old letters. One rainy day after my younger daughter had gone to school, I went down into the base- ment and got out my battered cardboard box of love letters. I brought it up to the bedroom and dumped it out on the bed. Then I remember putting on this old purple cardigan that had a rip at the elbow—it was a little cold—and I sat and read those letters. All of them: sweet, morning-after notes full of misspellings that Tom Winchell had taped onto my bathroom mirror; fountain-penned missives from Tim Stan- ley, who went on to study theology, and I know why—so he could stand in a pulpit and talk, talk, talk. I read things that made me get soft at the center again, that made me stare out the window and sigh. I got absolutely lost in reverie; I felt really out of it for hours after I'd finished reading those letters. I almost called one of my old boyfriends, but I could anticipate what would happen. I would pour out a rush of sentiment—"Now, this doesn't mean anything, but do you remember, do you remember the incredible *love* we felt for each other, do you remember when we stayed out all night to watch the sun come up by the river and you put your jacket around me and I had a cut on my lip and you kissed me so gently it made me think I could never, never leave you?" I'd say something like that and the now-balding Larry Drever, holding the phone at the desk from which he sells life insurance, would say, ". . . *Who* is this?"

So I know it's dangerous to reenter the past. Especially when things come back to you as strongly as they do to me. I'm extremely good at remembering, have had this ability since I was very young. Give me one rich detail, and I'll reconstruct a whole scene. Say "Dairy Queen," and I'll recall a night in high school when I was there with a bunch of friends and a cloud of gnats hung around Joe Antillo's head and he reached up to swat them away and spilled his root-beer float all over himself and Trudy Jameson, who was wearing a blue shirt tied at the waist, and jeans with one back pocket torn off and her silver charm bracelet and "Intimate" perfume. She had a cold that night. A few days earlier, her eight-year-old brother Kevin had fallen off his bicycle and cut his knee so badly he'd required seven stitches, half of which he removed later that night with his sister's manicure scissors—"just to see what would happen," he told his horrified parents when they drove him back to the emergency room. "How do you remember all these details?" people ask me all the time. I don't know how. I just do. One image leads to another, then another, as though they're all strung together. And in any given memory I summon up, I become again the person I was then—I feel the weather, I feel everything. I lose the person I am now to some other, younger self.

It can hurt you, remembering—the shock of reentry, the mild disorientation, the inevitable sadness that accompanies a true vision of the past. Still, right now, staring out the window at the land far below me, realizing I have no idea where I am, I want nothing more than to do absolutely that. I want to go back to the time when I started to lose my mother, and search for clues as to why and how. I suppose it's about time. I lean my seat back. Close my eyes. Begin.

ELIZABETH BERG's first novel, *Durable Goods*, was called "a gem" by Richard Bausch. Her other novels include *Talk Before Sleep, Range of Motion, The Pull of the Moon,* and *Joy School*. In 1997, she won the NEBA award for fiction. She lives in Massachusetts.

GONE FOR GOOD

Mark Childress

Dear BRC Reader,

Readers will never forget Lucille, the heroine of Mark Childress's *Crazy in Alabama*, who chops off her abusive husband's head, puts it in a hatbox, and takes off to California to become a star.

Now, in *Gone for Good*, Mark Childress's new novel, we are introduced to an equally unforgettable character. Ben "Superman" Willis is a superstar singer, who has it all, but just needs a break from it. His wish comes true when he lands on a desert island, which he decides must be Paradise when a woman who looks suspiciously like Marilyn Monroe sashays by. Soon he is hanging out with the likes of Amelia Earhart, Princess Anastasia and Jimmy Hoffa. But too much of anything can be a bad thing, and Superman soon finds that reality, no matter how tough, is sometimes better than fantasy.

Critics and readers alike have praised *Gone for Good*. Fannie Flagg said, "Proves once again that Mark Childress remains one of the most original and imaginative writers of our generation."

In this excerpt, our hero has just woken up with his body encased in a concrete cast and absolutely no idea where he is (or what he has gotten himself into).

Maureen O'Neal
Editorial Director,
Trade Paperbacks

In the dazzle of light, a wide straw hat cast its shadow over a face to remember: high, proud cheekbones, piercing hazel eyes, startling white eyelashes. A serene classical haughtiness that must have been left over from her youth, when she would have been handsome, not pretty. She was lanky and lean, knobby elbows and knees. She wore a man's white shirt, baggy khakis, embroidered Japanese slippers with fire-breathing dragons on the toes. She seemed tense, from her tight little smile to the precise way she held herself in the chair. Her arms and chest were deeply sun darkened and freckled, but her face was pink, in the shade of the hat, the wrinkles so soft the touch of a finger would make them disappear. She might be sixty years old, or eighty.

The man behind the wheelchair was old, too—small and stooped, with powerful shoulders and strong-muscled arms. He was an Indian, his face impassively flat-featured and forbidding, like one of those Mayan statues in the *National Geographic*.

The lady murmured a few words.

The old Indian stepped into the room behind Superman and at once produced a sound of pouring water. All the freshness and lightness and hope in the world were contained in that sound.

The old man came to the cot. Superman tipped his head up and drank from a brimming coconut shell.

If you awoke every morning knowing water would taste that good, you would leap up out of bed with a shout of joy.

"Cuidado, no le des demasiado," said the woman. The coconut was withdrawn. "We don't want to drown you."

Superman croaked, "You speak English?"

"Of course, I'm American. Sorry Gyp startled you—she's a sweet dog, once you get to know her. She's been watching over you night and day."

"How long . . . have I been here?"

"More than a month now." She wheeled closer to the bed. "God-amighty, that was a terrible ditch. I've seen some humdingers, but that was just about the worst. What were you trying to do, put her down in the lee of a wave? Whoever taught you to land in the lee of a wave? Didn't you see you had a nice long beach right there to land on?"

"Water," he croaked.

She nodded. The old man stepped forward. Superman gulped as much as he could before it was withdrawn.

"I suppose it's not very kind of me to criticize," she went on, "but I happened to be watching and I just wondered who put that idea in your head."

Superman considered it a real achievement to have landed a plane without wheels and lived to discuss it, but he didn't feel like discussing it at the moment with this old lady. He knew there was something important he needed to ask her, but he couldn't quite get his woozy consciousness wrapped around what it might be, so he settled for the obvious question: "Where am I?"

Her smile was gentle. "Where were you trying to go?"

"Phoenix."

"You're a long way from there. Who was your navigator?"

Superman shook his head. "Just me. I had some—instrument problems. I guess I wandered off course."

"What's your occupation? Surely you're not an aviator?"

"I'm a singer."

"That's how you make your living?"

"Yeah."

"Fine, you must hurry up and get well so you can sing for us."

Superman peered down at the concrete encasement. "Who did this to me?"

"That would be Pito," she said, with a little flourish of her hand. The old Indian bowed. "He's a natural genius at these sorts of things. Of course plaster would have been better than cement, but we had to make do. Is it awfully uncomfortable?"

"My arm," he said. "Can you—get him to pick up my arm?"

She translated. Pito lifted the concrete arm to the cot.

"What's wrong with my face? It hurts when I talk."

"There wasn't much we could do about that," the lady said. "Couldn't put your whole head in cement. You broke a lot of bones all over. I don't know how you looked before, but you look different now. Your name is Benjamin?"

"Ben," he said.

"Everyone calls me Emily. I think we should be friends. We have things in common. Tell me, Ben, where were you the last time you radioed your position?"

"I don't know. I was lost."

"Where did you think you were?"

"Mexico . . . ?"

"Well, that's fine. Now you need to rest. Pito, *la tintura*—"

Pito put a glass vial to Superman's lips. A sweet, heady flavor of flowers: ylang-ylang, jasmine, and others he didn't recognize, borne on a base of pure alcohol. A lovely floral-scented moonshine. Superman swilled it.

Pito tucked the vial away.

"Listen, lady," Superman said, "I've got a problem here."

"What's that?"

"You got my rear end wrapped up in cement. What happens when I have to, you know, go?"

"That's what's so ingenious about Pito's design. Pito, *traiga la manguera, el caballero quiere bañarse.*"

Pito came with a garden hose, which he inserted into a hole atop the concrete block. He winked at Superman, and went out again.

"What is he doing? He's not gonna—" Outside, a faucet squealed. The hose wriggled on the floor. Water came blasting down into the block, flooding his nether regions with a wicked chill. He set up a shout that brought the black dog into the house, barking.

Emily snapped her fingers. The dog dropped its head and lay down. Water drained out through a pipe in the floor.

"I'll bet that feels lovely," she said. "It's awfully hot today, even for here."

Superman wondered if he had fallen into the hands of madmen. "Lady, I want you to tell me where the hell I am."

"I can't, Ben. If I tell you, you won't be permitted to leave." She delivered this news without the first hint of a smile.

"What did you say?"

"This is a private island. Uninvited guests are invited to leave. As soon as you're in shape to travel, we'll get you out of here and back to the other world. Just don't ask a lot of questions and you'll be fine." She patted the concrete block. "At least you won't be wandering around poking your nose into things."

"Which . . . which ocean are we in? Atlantic or Pacific?"

"My, we were lost, weren't we? I'm serious, Ben. No questions. If you want to leave, you have to trust me to help you. Your ignorance will help me do that. Of course maybe you'll like it here and want to stay. It has been known to happen. It'd be nice to have a singer. Do you know 'Moonlight in Vermont'?"

"What happened to my plane?"

She shook her head. "Too bad about that. The natives are wonderful people, but if you leave something lying about, they think you must not want it. They were carting the pieces away before Pito got you out from under. He managed to save most of your things. . . . I was studying that electronical compass of yours. That's a beautiful piece of equipment."

"Yeah, it works great," said Superman. "I thought I was going to Phoenix." The taste of flowers lingered on his tongue, and now his mind was sidestroking pleasantly through the sultry air. "What was that stuff you gave me?"

"A sleeping potion. Nectars and bark infusions. Pito's recipe."

"Listen, you can't just . . . you gotta . . ." He blinked, and smiled. "Wow, it's pretty trippy, huh?" The air in the room shimmered and rippled.

Emily placed her hand on his arm. "Sleep," she commanded.

Superman closed his eyes and fell back into that dreamland where he had been keeping himself.

The bird sang while he slept. The rest of the song filled itself in. He awoke when the sun was very late, or very early. He recognized the song, and laughed out loud.

Whoo hoo hoo
Hoo hoo?
Whoo hoo hoo
Hoo hoo!
Uh, Louie Louie, oh, no,
sayin' we gotta go.
Yeah, yeah, yeah, yeah, yeah.

In a place where an old lady and her Indian medicine man wrap your ass in a loaf of concrete, and sedate you with nectar of flowers, it should not come as a surprise that a bird might be singing the first four bars of "Louie Louie." The lead guitar line.

Superman had not made it to paradise, not yet. But neither did this seem like quite the same old earth.

Suddenly he remembered what he had forgotten to ask. His delight melted into anger. His yell roused the dog to furious barking just past the bamboo wall. He called it a goddamn sonofabitch dog and told it to shut the hell up.

The bamboo wall slid back. Superman roared, "Go get her and bring her to me!" The old Indian gulped and beat a retreat. Apparently he understood English if you spoke it loud enough.

In two minutes the wheelchair came squealing up the path. Superman tried to pull up on his elbows to face her, but couldn't find the strength.

Her hair all askew. An embroidered kimono over rumpled red-striped pajamas. "What on earth is the matter with you?"

"What did you do with the money?" Superman demanded. "I had a lot of money in that plane. Where is it?"

"Why, you ungrateful—how dare you! Do you realize it's five o'clock in the morning? For God's sake, it's in the safe at my house."

That was not the answer he expected. He felt like an instant fool. "Oh . . . well, hell, why didn't you tell me?"

"I suppose I was more concerned with saving your life. You don't seem very appreciative. You seem to think we're *all* thieves." She sent Pito off with three words. "I knew this was trouble, bringing you here. But I really didn't have a choice, did I? I couldn't leave you to die. And this is the thanks I get."

"Lady, what did you expect me to think? You said they took my plane apart. You didn't say anything about my money."

"If you'd just *listen* instead of leaping to conclusions—I told you Pito saved some of your things, papers and some of the instruments, a guitar, that sack with all the cash. The guitar is broken. He's been trying to fix it for you."

"Look, I'm sorry, just—you haven't told me where I am, or who you are, or . . ."

"Those are not things you need to know."

"I gotta get out of here," he said. "I've got a kid, and, and a wife, and a career . . . I've got friends. They'll be looking for me."

"You'd be amazed how quickly they forget."

"You can't just keep me here. I'm famous, okay?" He hadn't wanted to play that card, but there it was, on the table.

She stared at him coolly. "I've never heard of you."

He puffed up a bit. "My name's Ben Willis. They call me Superman. I've got six gold records, okay? They're not gonna stop looking for me."

"In time they will."

He mulled the certainty with which she said that.

"But you should be up and out of here before then," she said, an afterthought.

Pito appeared with a tray, steaming saucepans of coffee and milk, two coconut shells. The dog followed him in.

"On the beach, when I crashed," Superman said. "I saw Marilyn Monroe."

Emily tasted her coffee. A smile crinkled the corners of her eyes. "Really?"

"She asked if I was dead. And she said I was kind of cute."

Pito proffered a shell filled with coffee and milk. Superman craned over to the paper straw and took a sip: hot and dark, with a flavor like burnt chocolate.

"That's quite a dream," said Emily.

"It wasn't a dream," Superman said. "She was real."

"Her name is Daisy. I've never seen any of the Marilyn Monroe movies, but everyone says the resemblance is uncanny."

He thought about that for a moment. He turned it over in his mind. "It wasn't a resemblance. It's her. She's not a blonde anymore. I heard her voice. I had a real good look at her."

She laughed, lightly. "You're not the first person to think so."

She was a bad liar, he thought—especially this early in the morning, with the crease of the pillow still in her face.

"That's what you don't want me to see," he said softly. "That is how Churming Dean she's here."

"Oh, Ben, that's silly." Her smile seemed frozen. "You took a pretty good bump on the head."

"How did she do it, how'd she get here? I mean, she's dead. They had a funeral and everything."

"Obviously it's impossible." She clasped the kimono to her throat. "You should really try to eat something today. You've lost too much weight."

"I know what I saw," he insisted.

She raised two fingers. The old man moved behind her chair. "We'll mash up some fruit for you, I think you can tolerate that," she said, gliding out. "If it doesn't rain, we'll open the house up later on and give you some air."

Superman sank back in wonder. He had fallen in love with Marilyn Monroe as she sashayed up the aisle of the train in *Some Like It Hot*. The day she died, he was driving from Birmingham to Gadsden to sing in a bar called the Cattle Drive. The news came over the radio. They played "Diamonds Are a Girl's Best Friend" then went back to their regular rotation. Ben pulled in at a roadhouse, got drunk, felt sad the whole day, missed the gig. She was a suicide, in a bungalow. The housekeeper found her lying naked across the bed. The coroner said sleeping pills. What a waste! Superman imagined that every American man spent that day grieving over the death of his secret dream—the dream that he, Mr. Joe Hot Blood Average Guy, would one day have his chance to make love to Marilyn Monroe.

And now she was here, in this place. One hundred percent alive. He knew it was true because the old lady kept her eyes down while she lied.

He smiled to himself. He had picked an interesting place to crash.

© JERRY BAUER

MARK CHILDRESS was born in Alabama, grew up in the Midwest and the South, and graduated from the University of Alabama. His articles and reviews have appeared in *The New York Times*, the *Los Angeles Times*, the *San Francisco Chronicle*, the *Times Literary Supplement*, *Southern Living*, and the *Birmingham News*, among other publications. He is the author of three children's books and four previous novels: *A World Made of Fire, V for Victor, Tender*, and *Crazy in Alabama*. He lives in Manuel Antonio, Costa Rica.

THE EDGE OF HEAVEN

Marita Golden

Dear BRC Reader,

Marita Golden has long been considered a "writer's writer"—a critically acclaimed treasure in the fertile field of African American women's fiction, who many readers have yet to discover. In *The Edge of Heaven*, she has written her most powerful novel—a compelling human drama about an African American family at its most vulnerable moments of love, violence, grief, and finally redemption. Reminiscent in emotional pitch of Anna Quindlen's bestselling novels, *One True Thing* and *Black and Blue*, Golden is in top form as she explores the deep and sometimes unresolvable issues that stretch the delicate weave of family relationships almost beyond endurance. Lee Smith likened this novel to *Snow Falling on Cedars*, and praised it as "Much more than a work of mystery, more than a novel about the effects of a past crime. It's a psychological page turner . . . Each believable character is deeply imagined and fully developed; each chapter pulls the reader straight into the next."

    The Edge of Heaven is unforgettable.

Cheryl Woodruff
Associate Publisher
One World

My mother returned that summer from an exile both imposed and earned. Nothing had prepared me for her departure. I was unsure how to claim her homecoming. But I share her talent for perseverance, for we are joined by more than I can bear. My mother came back to recognition and reckoning. I thought she came home to me.

At ten minutes after seven the morning of her return, it was already eighty-five degrees according to the deejay on the all-news radio station that woke me up.

All news, all the time, the station promised and delivered, and so even as I lay, partially asleep, poised to wake, I learned that the pollution and humidity made it a bad day for breathing and that the body of a young pregnant Black woman had been found in a park in Northeast Washington the night before. She had been stabbed and bludgeoned.

My cynicism was ornate and entirely deserved so I knew that only someone who thought they loved her could have unleashed such a torrent of rage. What had happened to us, my mother, my father, my grandmother, and me, had not dampened my curiosity about death, but perversely seemed to stoke it. If I saw a traffic accident in which the cars had been reduced to metallic rubble, I'd linger long after others had departed. The yellow police tape enclosing the scene was not a border, but simply a line to be crossed in my imagination. Standing before the carnage, I could never decide who was luckier, the covered, lifeless bodies on stretchers (the white sheets draped but never covering everything so that a foot or a shoe or the top of a head cheated anonymity), or those suffering pain, bruises, injury, but still alive.

Did she and her assailant argue in the park? I wondered of the dead woman as I rolled over and reached behind me to turn the volume down and switch to the soulful early morning gossip, music, and banter of WHUR, or was she murdered someplace else and her body dumped near the picnic tables? Lying on my back, I felt my hands roaming the terrain of my body, as though propelled by thoughts of their own. Once my palms and fingers confirmed limbs, skin, the tautness of my stomach, the veins in my neck, a sigh of relief fled my heart. A storm had awakened me in the middle of the night. The thunder clamored and menaced. But as an aggressive sunlight filtered into my room that morning, I wanted to know if the young woman was already dead when the rain began. Did the storm revive even a moment of her life? Did she open her mouth to whisper for help, only to have raindrops clog her throat?

My lavender sheets were humid and musty and my body grew numb each time I thought of my feet hitting the floor. My mother was coming home. And though I was terrified by the thought, the night before, within the boundaries of slumber, my mother's face spilled forth like a comforting hallucination, one induced by the potent alchemy of desire.

I lay in bed until seven-thirty, the numbers on the illuminated digital clock radio a neon countdown. When I finally got up, it was because I realized that my mother might arrive earlier than she had told us. Delay on my part would give her an advantage. I did not want to be caught, unawares, in the glare of my mother's love. Premeditated affection is what she would offer. I wanted a chance to choreograph my response too.

Drying off in front of the bathroom mirror, I confronted my face. It was then, as it is now, my mother's face. Undeniably hers. We share a curvature around the jawline that defines our visage, in the estimation of others, as unremitting, even stern. But for us both, I know, there was mostly reticence trembling beneath those bones. It was an unremarkable face, the only striking feature being the thick brows we shared, their natural arc softening what the jawline seemed to imply.

I applied more makeup than usual, my hands trembling and unsure as I lined my eyes and brushed on a thick coat of mascara, hoping to erase any hint of my mother's imprint. I had hoped to create a mask. My inept artistry had merely sharpened and clarified just how much I was her child. After I dressed I walked down the hall and knocked on my grandmother's bedroom door.

"Come in," she called softly. A proliferation of plants and flowers, philodendrons and wandering Jew, African violets, even a miniature cactus, made entering Ma Adele's room comparable to stepping into a rain forest. Some days I had heard her behind her door conversing with the plants. She had named the cactus Butch and the azaleas that hung from the ceiling Aretha.

"I just got through talking to your mother a few minutes ago. Didn't you hear me calling you?" My grandmother sat enthroned in the king-sized bed among half a dozen pillows, her white hair uncombed, her purple and green floral robe open, exposing the wrinkled crevice between her breasts.

"I was in the shower," I told her as I sat on the foot of her bed, the gently perfumed scent of the pink hyacinths in bloom on her nightstand, the eucalyptus stationed in the window, making me slightly dizzy. "I didn't hear you."

"Well, it would've been nice if you could've spoken to her," she said, dismissing my defense with a skeptical glance over the tops of her bifocals as she thumbed through *The Daily Word*. "You come straight home from work this evening, you hear?"

"Yes ma'am."

"Straight home."

The TV remote control, a paperback mystery, an aged, tattered leather phone book, knitting needles, a ball of yarn, and a stack of bills littered my grandmother's bed. I saw as well a pile of letters from my mother. The sight of my mother's handwriting—small, precise, and legible, so unlike my own, ignited a keen spark of longing I could almost taste. The letters lay spread like a fan. The envelopes had been slit open neatly and remained white and crisp. Where had my grandmother stored them?

The letters my mother had written me had ragged envelope tops, for I had impatiently, even brutally, pried them open with my thumb the days I came home from school to find them on my bed. The pages were grimy, laden with fingerprints, and crinkled, as though they had lived a lifetime in my hands. I stored them in my desk drawer with my diary, pens, school assignments, phone numbers, spare change, loose earrings, photos of friends, verses from poems I had written, and a broken Timex watch. There the letters mingled with the other secrets I wished I could tell.

"How do you feel? Now that she's coming home?"

"I'm just glad it's over," my grandmother said, her voice thick with weariness. Yet I heard beneath that familiar sound the simmering, satisfied whisper of anticipation.

"Teresa, it's time to move on."

"Just like that?"

"Your mother's coming home expecting to find a daughter here. Don't disappoint her."

"And what do I get?" A ripple of nausea crossed the plain of my stomach.

"You get your mother back. You're not the only one who suffered, Teresa, she suffered worst of all."

"Do you really think *she* suffered worst of all, do you really believe that?"

"She lost everything."

"I did too. What do I do with everything I feel?" Clumps of sickness congealed in the pit of my stomach as I bit my tongue and bunched it at the back of my throat to keep from throwing up.

"You let it go. She'll need you to love her, love her to the bone."

"I need the same thing."

"Don't turn this into a contest, to see who needs more. You ought to be glad you still have a mother."

"I haven't had a mother since she left. I won't automatically have one when she comes back."

"Don't bring that attitude into this house tonight, you hear?" she warned me, her hands suddenly implacable, serious, stationed on her hips, a sign I had slipped into deep waters.

"What if it's all I've got?" I whimpered.

"I don't believe that. Neither do you."

My grandmother's understanding edged toward me like a malevolent impulse I dared not trust. Bolting from her bed, I ran from the room, ignoring her pleas for me to come back. Before her there was nothing I could hide. Even in my flight there was nowhere really to run.

On the front porch I closed the door behind me and slumped against it for several minutes. Finally I braved a step off the porch. The grasp of the sun was punishing as I walked down the hill toward Fourteenth Street to catch the bus, wondering not when but if this day would end.

* * *

The cabdriver was from Afghanistan. His broken English sputtered like an enticing but dense and nearly indecipherable song as he explained to Lena that he had been in America two weeks, and driving a taxi for three days. Not long after she settled in the backseat, Lena discovered that Mohammed Amin—she saw his name beside his picture on the sun visor above the front passenger seat—could not have found his way to the White House if it were three blocks away. Panic clouded the cabdriver's dark, bearded face as he repeatedly asked Lena for directions to her mother's Ingraham Street address. With a broad sweep of his hands, the cabdriver generously urged, "You show me way. You show me way."

Lena told him the most direct route and then huddled in the backseat, surveying the streets of a strangely unfamiliar downtown. Sleek new office buildings were rooted on nearly every corner. The buildings' colorful facades, tinted windows, and offbeat symmetry was playful yet resolute. The architecture deconstructed the awesome self-consciousness, the longing for grandeur and empire that studded the columns of the federal buildings that had always invested the city with a slightly grim demeanor. These new buildings were quirky, yet they too spoke of commerce and contracts. What else had changed, Lena wondered even as she remembered that Teresa worked in a building like the ones they passed. It was three o'clock. Inside some hermetically sealed office was Teresa swamped with work or in the middle of an afternoon break. Was she eager to come home that evening, or plotting, even in the midst of her job, some insurrection to greet her return?

During the bus ride through the craggy hauntingly eloquent mountains of West Virginia, Lena had slept. The thought of what awaited her frightened Lena so that she slept hard and deep most of the ride down as a defense against the encroachment of thoughts of what she longed for and feared most—home. What was there to sleeping? You closed your eyes, but then your subconscious woke up, went on foot patrol across your mind. It was nearly a year after Kenya's death before something like slumber returned, rest without pills, without the fear that despite the pills she would not sleep, fear pumping her so full of anxiety that she lay awake, energized and anxious until dawn. Retrieving that skill, that blessed ability, she had spent long hours in her room prone, feigning a kind of temporary death, sleeping just because she could. Now she was groggy, headachy, betrayed by sleep that had offered escape but not rest.

* * *

Just as she raised her hand to knock, Adele's brisk, purposeful footsteps filled the hallway. As Lena heard the noisy, metallic, foreboding sound of the two locks being turned, she envisioned her mother dismantling the safety net that Adele Ramsey, like everyone, hoped would keep disaster at bay or drive it to someone else's door.

"Well, it's about time, I was getting worried," Adele said, hugging Lena, engulfing her in the overwhelming scent of a thick cologne.

"I had a cabdriver from Afghanistan. He didn't know how to get here." Now that she was inside the house, Lena longed to be outside once again.

"Afghanistan?" Adele asked as she placed Lena's suitcase beside the coffee table.

"It's in Asia, Mama, near Pakistan."

"Last year, when Loretta and I came back from the Bahamas, we arrived at Dulles and had a cabdriver from Iran," Adele said with a dismayed shake of her head. She settled on the sofa, watching Lena stand for several seconds beside a chair, her eyes scanning the room as if searching for clues to where she was. An expectant, tense moment blossomed between the two women. Finally Lena sat down, tossing her purse onto the floor next to her chair.

"How was the ride down?"

"Exhausting."

"You look good."

"You sound surprised."

"I didn't know what to expect. It's been a while since we visited you last."

"I went on a diet a few weeks ago, started running in the morning. It was important for me to come back looking better than people would expect."

"Don't mind people."

"Are you saying you never did?"

"I'm saying you don't owe anybody any excuses or anything you don't want to tell."

"What's left to tell? What's left that anybody doesn't know?" Lena shrugged.

"More than you think," Adele said gently.

"What time will Teresa be home?"

"Around six."

"I'm almost afraid to see her."

"I'm just glad you're finally back."

"I ran into Ellington James as I was getting out of the cab."

"It's a shame about his father. A college professor and now he can't even remember his own name," Adele said wistfully. "And Daniel Jackson, who lived at the end of the block, he died last year of a stroke."

"You told me, Mama."

The upwardly mobile strivers who had purchased the houses thirty, sometimes forty, years ago were passing into illness and death, swept there by a force that would claim her one day too, Lena thought. She did not want to know the names of anyone else who had died while she was away or been crippled by some awesome, incurable disease. She knew she would have to visit Ellington's father. But what could she possibly say that he would hear or understand? How could she look at him and not wonder if she was looking at who she might one day be?

"What has it meant, Mama, all these years to have this house?" She asked the question, moving from her chair to sit beside Adele on the plush navy blue velveteen sofa, longing to sit so close to her mother she might hear her heart beat, feel the warmth of her breath.

But before Adele could answer, Lena spoke the words she had tried to exorcise since she woke that morning. "What do I do now? Mama, I've got nothing left of my life." Finally she had said the words, but felt only terror, felt them gagging her, twisting her arms behind her back. The question languished in the air as both verdict and destiny.

"Lena, you know I never had a lot of time for pity parties. You've got your health, Teresa, and you've got no time to waste on feeling sorry. If you want pity, then maybe you should stay someplace else," Adele told her with a steely calm.

Then she stood up and began walking around the room, straightening the objects on the mantel, the magazines atop the television, clearly liberated by the distance she had placed between her daughter and herself.

"Do you think it was easy for me?" she asked, continuing to pace. "I'm seventy years old. To raise a teenager, at my age? I wouldn't have had it any other way. Ryland could hardly get through the day after you left, much less be responsible for Teresa. But I had already raised you. I didn't plan on raising any children again."

Standing before the picture window, Adele's hands smoothed the bodice of her crisp salmon-colored sleeveless dress, the movements offering the comfort that, Lena could now see clearly, her mother never got any other way.

"And I lost my granddaughter, lost her in some way none of us can explain. It's terrible to lose your grandbaby, Lena." Adele's soliloquy gained fervor in the room's appalling quiet. She might have been addressing a gathering of ghosts lined up on the other side of the window. "That's what Kenya was. She was my baby too because she came out of you and you came out of me. You didn't grieve alone. And you weren't in prison by yourself."

Adele turned around but did not look at her daughter, avoided Lena's eyes as she continued her reconnaissance of the room, tinkering, puttering with the scores of ceramic objects and photos on the tables.

"And losing you." She shook her head. "Those visits to Farmingham just made it worse. I was afraid every day something would happen to you there. Something more awful than what already had. The calls, the visits, the letters—they never put my fears to rest."

Having circumnavigated the room, she found herself once again sitting beside Lena. "What happened was terrible. And now we all have to go on."

"I'm sorry," Lena said, wiping her eyes, recomposing herself.

"Maybe what you need is understanding." Adele relented slightly, her eyes resting on Lena, narrowed in bold assessment.

"I'll try to understand. But I want you more than anything to have faith, Lena. In yourself. You had a good life before this happened. Doubt didn't take you there, belief did.

"You'll have to go on from here, from this awful place, even if you don't know the way," Adele said . . .

The author of three other novels, *And Do Remember Me*, *Long Distance Life*, and *A Woman's Place*, MARITA GOLDEN has also written *Migrations of the Heart* and *Saving Our Sons: Raising Black Children in a Turbulent World*; edited *Wild Women Don't Wear No Blues: Black Women Writers on Men, Love, and Sex*; and coedited *Skin Deep: Black Women and White Women Write About Race*. She is the executive director of the Zora Neale Hurston/Richard Wright Foundation.

HANNA'S DAUGHTERS

Marianne Fredriksson

Dear BRC Reader,

Hanna's Daughters is the story of three generations of Swedish women—a grandmother, a mother, and a daughter—and it spans 100 years of Scandinavian history. It reminded me of *The Joy Luck Club* and *Wild Swans*, two books that bring you deep inside another culture, yet deal with universal themes.

In *Hanna's Daughters*, these themes are the often difficult but enduring ties between mothers and daughters, the sacrifices, compromises, and rewards in the relationships between men and women, and the patterns that repeat themselves through generations.

Though I know little about Scandinavia, these characters felt so familiar to me, and I missed them and thought about them long after I had finished the book. I even called my mother and began to ask her about her mother—my grandmother—whom I had never known. I hope that you read *Hanna's Daughters* and are moved to discover more about your own roots and family patterns, and that you too will consider yourself one of *Hanna's Daughters*.

In the first excerpt, we find Anna, the granddaughter, wondering about her grandmother, whom she feels she never really knew. In the second excerpt, we learn more about Hanna, the grandmother, and her difficult early life.

Maureen O'Neal
Editorial Director,
Trade Paperbacks

The golden light woke her early. Perhaps not just the light, for in her dreams she'd heard birdsong from the garden, as lovely and strong as the spring itself. For a moment she lay still, trying to distinguish the voices, the chaffinch's joy, the cheerful signals of blue tits, and the whirr of swallows as they flew low in toward the eaves.

The swallows have arrived and are building their nests under the eaves, she thought, for a moment able to feel that everything was as it should be.

She slipped down to the kitchen, and as soundlessly as a ghost she got herself a cup of coffee, stole a cinnamon bun, and crept silently back upstairs, remembered that the sixth stair creaked and success-fully stepped over it. The old man snored in the bedroom.

She meditated, the birdsong assisting her into her own silence and the knowledge that nothing is harmful even if all is suffering. For a while, she even succeeded in thinking things weren't too bad for her mother, that she had gone beyond pain. And that her father's memory was so short, he couldn't keep up his bitterness.

Then she took out the photograph of her grandmother and gazed at it for a long time.

Hanna Broman. Who are you? I knew you, oddly enough, almost only from hearsay. You were a legend, magnificent and questionable. So amazingly strong, Mother said.

I must have images of my own. You lived until I was an adult, a wife, and a mother. But the photograph bears no resemblance to my memories of you. That's understandable. The photo was taken when

you were young, a woman in her best years. I saw you only as old,
a stranger, tremendously large, enveloped in huge pleated black
dresses.

So this is what you looked like in the days of your strength, when
you walked six miles with a fifty-kilo sack of flour from the mill to the
village on the border. There you bartered with it for coffee, paraffin,
salt, and other necessities.

Can it be true? You carried the heavy sack on your back, Mother
said. But only in spring and autumn. In the summer you rowed, and
in winter you pulled a sled across the ice.

We were born into different worlds, you and I. But I can see now
we are alike, the same forehead and the same jagged hairline. The
same broad mouth and short nose. But you don't have my chin, no,
yours is strong and obstinate. Your gaze is steady, your eyes keeping
their distance. I remember they were brown.

Anna looked into Hanna's eyes for a long time. She thought, we're
looking at each other for the first time ever.

Who were you? Why did we never get to know each other? Why
were you so uninterested in me?

Suddenly Anna heard a question, the child who said, "Why isn't
she a proper gran? Whose lap you can sit on and who tells stories?"

And her mother's voice. "She's old and tired, Anna. She's had
enough of children. And there was never any time for stories in her
life."

Was there bitterness in that voice?

I must go to what I myself remember.

When Anna was small and Grandmother was still able to walk the
long way from the bus stop to the house by the sea where Anna's
family lived, Grandmother sometimes came to see them in the mornings. She sat on the kitchen sofa in the aroma of cakes and newly
baked bread, and the table was laid with a fine cloth and the best
cups. She brought comfort with her, like a cat settling in the corner of
a sofa and purring. She purred, too, Anna remembered, creaking like
a corncrake at night. When she wasn't talking.

Even her talk brought pleasure, a strange language, half Norwe-
gian, easygoing, sometimes incomprehensible.

"Us here," she said. "Indeed, that's it." She always succeeded in
surprising herself and others because her words flew out of her

mouth before she had time to think. Then she looked surprised and stopped abruptly, shamefaced or laughing.

What had they talked about?

Their neighbors in the block. About children it had gone badly for, about men who drank and women who were ill. But also about weddings and new children born and parties and food and however could people afford it.

For the child, Anna, it was like lifting the roof off a dollhouse and seeing crowds of people. Like a game. But for the two women, it was reality, and serious. They had a living interest in the Höglunds' delicate children, and Johansson the master painter's boozing. Not to mention Mrs. Niklasson's peculiar illness.

Gossip. Not malicious, nor kindly. For the first time, Anna thought now that the endless talk was an orgy of emotions. They wallowed in the misfortunes of others, tut-tutted and lived out their personal needs without ever becoming personal. Talking about yourself was impossible. Shameful.

Grandmother flushed easily.

"Don't you ever cry, Gran?"

"No. No point," she said, flushing scarlet.

Mother was also embarrassed and scolded the child. There was a lot you couldn't ask Grandmother, who probably thought impertinent children should be reprimanded and that Johanna's spoiled daughter had no manners.

"You were so damned practical," Anna said to the photograph.

Perhaps I'm wrong, she thought as she turned her eyes away from the photo to look beyond the window, past all those small houses where anonymous people lived wall to wall and scarcely even knew each other by name. Perhaps you both had a sorrowful longing back to the village you came from. And you were trying to restore the connection and the village feeling when you came to the big city.

Anna could hear her grandmother snorting at that explanation. She liked the city, the electric light and running water, the nearby shops, and the right to close your own door.

Grandmother would come for Sunday dinner. Dad fetched her in the car, and she wore long black jet necklaces and white ruffles at her throat. She said nothing at the table until addressed, and was always submissive to her son-in-law.

Anna suddenly remembered, a perfectly clear memory, she thought with surprise. All around the dinner table were amazed voices turning over and over the schoolmistress's words about Anna being gifted.

Gifted? That was an unusual word. The teacher had talked about high school. Grandmother flushed and snorted, finding the talk indecent. She took a long look at the girl and said, "What use'd that be? She ain't nothing but a girl. She'd get superior and it'd come to nothing."

Perhaps those were the words that settled Anna's future. "Nothing but a girl" had aroused her father's anger. He, who would otherwise never admit to his grief over his only child being a girl.

"Anna'll have to decide for herself," he said. "If she wants to go on at school, she's to do so."

How had I forgotten that Sunday, that conversation, Anna thought, going back to bed and looking at the photograph again. You were wrong, you old witch, she thought. I went on at school, I took exams, I was successful and moved in worlds you couldn't even dream of.

I became superior, too, just as you said, as everyone said. And as far as you're concerned, you became a fossil, a primitive leftover from a vanished time. I excluded you from my life. You were a painful reminder of origins I was ashamed of.

That's why I never got to know you and have no memory of you. But it's also why your photograph speaks so strongly to me. For it says quite clearly that you were a gifted girl, too.

Your prejudices were different from mine, that's true. But you were right sometimes, especially when you said that I wouldn't get away, either. For me, too, a woman's life awaited me.

I didn't carry sacks of flour from the mill to the village, Grandmother. And yet I did.

Hanna's mother had two batches of children. The first four died in the famine in the late 1860s. Maja-Lisa marked time, daring to believe she would have no more.

But in 1870, spring came with rain, just as it should, the baked soil drank, and once again there was bread on the table. There was no talk of surplus, but by autumn they had turnips and potatoes in the earth cellar and cows that had grazed enough to give milk once again.

And Maja-Lisa was with child.

She cursed her fate, but August, her husband, said they should be grateful. The bad years hadn't driven them from the farm and they

hadn't had to wander the roads as vagrants in gypsy carts like so
many other farmers in Dalsland.

Hanna was the eldest child in the new batch, then along came another girl and three boys. Her mother had learned from the famine
never to get fond of a new child. And to fear dirt and bad air.

The latter she'd learned in church.

In the days before the famine years, they'd had a young gentle-
eyed priest who did his best to live in the imitation of Christ. He
shared his bread with the old, and wherever he went, he had milk
with him for the children, although the parsonage itself was also
short of food. In the daytime, he buried children and the old and
signed papers for all those fleeing west to Norway and America. At
night he prayed for his poor people.

As his prayers had no visible effect, he instead more and more frequently took to writings he had been given by his brother, a doctor in
Karlstad. That was how his sermons came to be about the importance
of cleanliness. The consumption thrived in dirt, and rickets in the
darkness, he told them. All children should be out in the daylight.
They didn't die of cold, but of darkness and filth, he thundered. And
they had to have milk.

It was a message his congregation would have scorned if times
had been ordinary. But now the mothers listened with anxiety, and
Maja-Lisa took his talk about cleanliness seriously.

There was trouble at home as she persuaded her husband not to
spit on the rag rugs. But she was relentless, for she found the priest
was right. Her new children were unusually strong and healthy.

But the gentle-eyed priest left and was replaced by one given to
drink. With the change of priest, as with most things in the district,
worse was to come after the famine years. Fear had settled in, and joy
was in short supply, but there was plenty of envy. Distances between
houses also grew, as the forest took over the fields and meadows
around abandoned farms.

And in winter, the procession of beggars straggled through the
villages, reminding them all.

When Hanna was ten, the new priest came to Bråten to hear their
catechism and told them they ought to thank God for being allowed

to live in such a beautiful place. Hanna looked with surprise over the lake and the high mountains. She didn't understand what the priest was talking about. Even less did she grasp what he meant when he assured her God took care of his children. God helped only those with hard hands, those who learned to save every crumb.

At twelve, the girl was sent into service at the farm on the river mouth. She had been at school long enough to be able to write and do sums. That was enough, her father said.

Lyckan, as the farm was called, was ruled by Lovisa, a mean woman, known for her harshness and arrogance. The farm was considered rich in these poverty-stricken areas. Elsewhere, it would have been a pitifully small farm. Lovisa was unlucky with her children, two infant daughters crushed to death, and a son who also died, shrunken and crippled with rickets. Now only one was left, a handsome boy, used to having his own way. He was not like ordinary folk, even in appearance; he was dark and black-eyed.

Malicious tongues talked about the gypsy tribe that had come through the district the summer before he was born. But sensible people reminded themselves that Lovisa's grandfather was Spanish, a shipwrecked sailor rescued off the coast.

The farms were related. Joel Eriksson at Lyckan was Maja-Lisa's brother. Hanna's maternal grandfather, Erik Eriksson, still lived at the main farm, Framgården, but had shared his outlying farms between the children. Joel, the son, was given the large farm of Lyckan. Maja-Lisa and her husband had to be tenants at Bråten, a poorer and smaller farm.

As if nonetheless there was some justice in life after all, Maja-Lisa had a good and hardworking husband in August Olsson, born and bred in Norway, while the son Joel was stuck with the difficult Lovisa from Bohuslän.

Lovisa was pious. Like many of that kind, she delighted in keeping her fellow human beings in the good graces of the Lord and with good conscience was able to indulge daily in being cruel.

By now, Hanna was used to long days, hard work, and much abuse. So she didn't complain and never knew the neighbors pitied her, saying Lovisa worked her like a beast of burden. The girl had enough to eat and once a month she was happy. That was when she went home to her mother with a bushel of flour.

When the darkness closed in, in October, she menstruated. It hurt. She bled a great deal and was frightened, but didn't dare go to Lovisa. She took her most worn shift, tore it into strips, and squeezed her legs together to keep the bloody rag in place.

Lovisa looked suspiciously at her, and shouted, "You moves like a knock-kneed heifer. Get a move on, girl."

Not until Hanna got back home to her mother on Saturday could she cry, and then only slightly, for her mother as usual said crying never did any good. But she got help with proper crocheted towels and a ribbon for around her waist. Two expensive safety pins were found in her mother's sewing box. She felt wealthy.

Then Maja-Lisa said, "Now you has to know it's dangerous. Never let no man closer than two ells from you."

Then came the evening at Lyckan when she fell asleep in the hay. She had her sleeping place in the kitchen, but there was no peace there with all the quarrels in the evenings, usually about the son the mother spoiled and the father wanted to make something of. Hanna was always so tired she was usually able to sleep despite the fearful words flying over the straw mattress in the servant's box-bed. But that evening, her master and mistress were fighting in the bedroom, and the sound of heavy blows and screams penetrated through to the kitchen. Hanna thought, now he's killing her, that Joel. But then she heard dark Rickard calling, a terrible agitated cry like a bellow from the underworld.

They've woken him, God help us.

She slipped out into the barn then, deathly frightened the boy would begin to pinch her the moment his mother's eyes were elsewhere.

She slept in the hay like an exhausted animal and didn't wake up until he was pulling at her skirt. She tried screaming, but he gripped her by the throat and she knew she was going to die. Faced with that, she lay still. He was as heavy as a bull as he hurled himself onto her, and when he thrust inside her and she broke, in all that hideous pain, she prayed to God to take her.

Then she died and was surprised when she woke an hour or so later, bloody and torn. She could move, first her hands, then her arms, and lastly her legs. Finally, she was able to make a decision, or at least shape a thought: home to Mother.

She walked slowly through the forest, leaving a bloodstained trail behind her. She crawled the last bit on all fours, but when she called out outside their door, her voice was loud enough to wake her mother.

For the first and only time in her life, Hanna saw her mother weep. The girl was put on the kitchen table, and her mother washed and washed, but was unable to stop the bleeding.

"Dear Lord," said Maja-Lisa, over and over again, before pulling herself together and sending her eldest boy for Anna, the midwife who had helped Maja-Lisa through her many deliveries. She was also good at stemming bleeding.

"Hurry, hurry!" she yelled at the boy.

Then when she was about to take off the girl's ripped clothing, she stopped. In her wild fury, she had remembered only that Anna was the midwife, but not that she was also the one who went from cottage to cottage with all the wicked secrets of the village.

Hanna was asleep, or unconscious; Maja-Lisa couldn't make out which. The kitchen looked like a slaughtering shed, and more and more vociferously she called upon God to show mercy, while the children around her put their hands over their ears and eyes.

Then Anna came at last, sturdy and calm. She had brought finely grated wild parsley and mixed rubella into it, then she greased the girl's loins with the ointment. The treatment woke Hanna, and slowly she began to weep.

The midwife leaned over the child and said, "Who?"

"Black Rickard," the girl whispered.

"Might've known," said Anna harshly. Then she gave the child a concoction of mistletoe and white deadnettle. "That should stop the bleeding and make you sleep like the dead," she said. "But God knows if you'll ever be able to have babes. And you won't never get married."

Maja-Lisa didn't look upset, nor had she any idea that Anna's two predictions would come to nothing. She sent the child off to bed in the other room, put on the coffee, cleaned up the kitchen, then noticed the shotgun had gone from the wall and August had vanished.

She screamed again. The children came racing out of the other room, but Anna had seen what Maja-Lisa had seen, and just snorted.

"Men! Calm down, woman. There ain't nothing we can do."

"He'll end up in the fortress," cried Maja-Lisa.

"I don't think he'll succeed."

She was right in that prediction. When August got to Lyckan, the son had disappeared. Both farmers calmed themselves with strong drink and decided that the boy should be forced into marriage as soon as Hanna was of marriageable age, and until then she was to be respected as a daughter in the house.

But nothing much came of the agreement. Hanna said she'd rather jump in the river than marry Rickard. Powerless, Maja-Lisa said nothing. Lovisa got secret messages to her son saying that for the sake of Jesus Christ, he must keep away from the farm; old Anna was talking about the police, saying that when she was small there'd been talk of a man condemned to death for despoiling a servant girl.

But neither August nor Maja-Lisa wanted to cause such vexation to the relatives at Lyckan.

Tongues wagged in the cottages. People began avoiding Lovisa and Lyckan. Until it was clear one day that Hanna was with child, and more and more came to the conclusion that she hadn't been all that unwilling. All the talk about her being so badly hurt was lies. Old Anna's tongue had run away with her, as usual.

MARIANNE FREDRIKSSON's novels have sold more than two million copies in her native Sweden. *Hanna's Daughters* is her first U.S. publication. Rights to *Hanna's Daughters* have been sold to twenty-seven countries, and the U.S. hardcover edition was a national bestseller.

By the Light of My Father's Smile

Alice Walker

Dear BRC Reader,

Pulitzer Prize winner Alice Walker is a boldly inventive writer whose work defies easy categorization. From *The Color Purple* to *Possessing the Secret Joy*, she always pushes against the boundaries of our imaginations and our comfortable, unexamined beliefs. In *By the Light of My Father's Smile*, her first novel in six years, Walker crosses conventional borders and lands us firmly in the terrain of writers like Isabelle Allende.

Susannah and Magdalena are two sisters who, along with their parents, join an endangered band of mixed-race Blacks and Indians called the Mundo. As Alice Walker herself puts it, the novel is "a celebration of sexuality, its absolute usefulness in the accessing of one's own spiritual maturity, and the father's role in assuring joy or sorrow in this arena for his female children." In this transcendent novel, Walker reminds us that "love is both timeless and beyond time," and that "sexuality is not evil but a blessing."

Cheryl Woodruff
Associate Publisher
One World

Twigs

I did not know until much later that Susannah was outside our bedroom door while Daddy was punishing me. It must have been as incomprehensible to her as it was to me. I knew I had disobeyed him, but he was after all a minister, or at least putting up a mighty show of being one. He'd even gradually graduated from pastor, wearing a plain tan colored suit on Sundays, to priest, and wore black every day. His profession, as he explained it to me and Susannah, was based on the forgiveness of other people's sins. In the long white dresses he ordered for me and the Mary Jane shoes, the quaint colorful shawls he purchased from the village weavers, I'm sure he thought me hobbled. But he did not understand my passion for riding horses, or my particular passion for riding Vado, the black stallion that belonged to Manuelito. And so, of course, he did not know where to look when it was clear I had escaped the nest. That from the look of things I had escaped at will, even while the door was locked. That even Susannah, his adoring flunky, had been in cahoots with me, and had lied to him. Oh, Daddy dear, as she sweetly and sickeningly called him, our Magdalena is sleeping. Oh, Daddy dear, our Magdalena is in the water closet. Oh, Daddy dear, she seems to have fainted from stomach cramps.

But on that last day I did not sneak. Manuelito and Vado appeared on a rise I could see from my window, and while the family ate lunch, I went out to them. I hitched my long skirt high up on my thighs and Manuelito swung down for me. We were equally brown, equally bold of dark and reckless eye. We'd been twin spirits since the day I arrived with my family so many years ago. And Manuelito had pinched me in the ribs while Daddy led his first froggy-throated prayer, a prayer he'd learned in the car on the way down and obviously didn't believe, and I'd promptly stepped on his bare foot—in my leather-soled North American shoes—hard.

It was like that with us. No tears, lots of pain. We did not speak of loving each other. No. That was not our way at all. We instead discovered bird's nests together, abandoned trails, poisoned wells, vulture feasts, rattlesnake beds, a valley of bluebells early in the spring. All these we shared almost wordlessly. And when we touched each other there was a casual ownership about it, an ownership that claimed just the moment of the actual touching, nothing more. But what this meant was that when Manuelito touched just one curl of my wayward hair—for in Mexico we were not bothered to straighten it—that one seemingly absentminded fingering was felt as something alive, curling, electric, as far down as my toes.

The place we went to was familiar. In fact, it was our home. We went home. We went to our house. I love to think of it this way even now. It was a shallow cave in the side of the mountains. A rusty shrub obscured our door. But from inside you could see through the shrub, and then our living room faced a valley. And it was in our yard that, in springtime, the wild bluebells grew.

We furnished our home with just a blanket, hidden behind some rocks, and a water jug, refilled from Manuelito's goatskin each time we came. In our home, I was called by my name, Magdalena. It was only in Manuelito's voice that it sounded right. He said it softly. With such respect! He said he liked the sound of it especially whispered, like a prayer, against my clitoris. When his mouth formed my name there, and I experienced the feathery movement of his breath, I felt my whole self seen. Everything in me, including everything in my soul, seemed to run into his arms. Manuelito, my love, my *angelito*, my pretty, pretty boy, I whispered back to him. And the light and the mountains and the bluebells . . . all of it was us.

I thought I could have become pregnant since I was fourteen, for that was the first time I lay down with Manuelito, himself one year my junior. But when I told him this later, he laughed and said no, that for one whole year we had fumbled blindly, for he had not known quite what to do. Everything we did pleased me, and I was fulfilled simply to lie close beside him and nibble at the corners of his mouth, or lick his eyelids. His lashes were so long that, when he closed his eyes, they appeared to be small black fans.

Maybe by fifteen years of age I might have embarrassed my father by carrying Manuelito's child. But by then his father and uncles and older brothers had taught him what all the young boys were taught during initiation: how not to impregnate anyone. I was safe. Worshipped is how it felt. To know myself so thought of, so cared about, to know that he would withdraw from me at just the right moment, no matter that I held him tight. To feel in myself and in my response to Manuelito such depths of trust and desire caused me to feel innately holy, as if our love made a magic circle about me that cloaked me in a private invisibility when I was obliged to return home.

Manuelito's soft tongue on my nipples, his soft words in my ear, his sturdy penis moving inside me. The beauty of his brown body above me, warming the shaded, sometimes quite chilly cave. The light that was drawn around the shrub guardian to suffuse our space. All these images I stored up for the time, later, when I would be in the North. A brown girl whose father was a minister and who had had the unusual experience of living years of her life in the faraway mountains of Mexico.

This time my father knew. I wonder if he'd known other times as well. For there was a craftiness, a streak of crafty meanness, in him. Perhaps he deliberately waited until we were about to leave the mountains before confronting me. Manuelito had given me a silver belt—rather, it was a leather belt that was covered with small silver disks. He'd made it himself. I kept it in bed with me, underneath my pillow. It was with this that my father punished me.

This is not an unusual story. I know that now. Fathers attack their children around the world, every day. But I did not know this then. I knew I was wild. Disobedient. Wayward and headstrong. But I did not understand his violence, after I had just experienced so much pleasure. So much sweetness. If he had known, if I could have told him, I felt he should have been happy for me. If in fact he loved me, as he often said he did. But no, he thrashed me in silence. I withstood it, in silence. I sent my spirit flying out the window to land on the glistening black back of Vado, my arms circling Manuelito's neat waist.

We flew along our favorite trail through the mountains, bluebells vibrant at our feet. Apparently Susannah sobbed for both of us. On her knees outside our bedroom, her eye to the keyhole; my mother behind her, packing with an air of righteous resignation. Once again, because of his stubborn behavior, she said, she was going to leave my father.

She never did.

After the beating she was warm to me and cool to him for several weeks. Then, it simply evened out again. The temperature in our house—the roomy, boxy one with the lawn, in Sag Harbor—became normal. He moved, finally, into the big bedroom where she slept alone at night. Sounds came from that room, voices, late into the night. Within a month, or less, my father loved my mother back to himself.

But something had happened to precious little Susannah at the keyhole. It was as if she'd peered into our simple, girlish bedroom through the keyhole and witnessed her gentle, compassionate father turn into Godzilla. She would never be loved back to her daddy again. With time, as I understood how severely the twig was bent in that moment of her horror and disbelief, my revenge against my father, a revenge so subtle Susannah would not realize its damage to her for another thirty years, was born. As for my father, he would never again be permitted to really know or enjoy his favorite little tree.

Twins

Susannah is writing a novel that explores the relationship she had with a man after her marriage to the Greek. But she is having difficulties. She cannot write in any sex. *Write it in,* I screech from the celestial sidelines. *Put the sex right on up in there!* Even if it's nothing but the copulating dogs you saw from your window as a five-year-old when we lived in Mexico: you thought they were twins, that being hooked together in that way was what being twins meant. Your mother and I laughed, and I remember thinking that even your little mind was cute. Or think of the giraffes you saw doing it years later in Africa, their long necks like chimneys. You stared, and started to fan yourself. Your lover smiled to himself. That night he shocked and stirred you, when he entered you from behind. It is not so big a deal! I want her to know. As I see her, crippled in a place that should be free, and still, after all these years, perplexed by the memory of her sister's stubborn face and the sound of the whistling silver belt. And my own face, what did she read there, what message about the consequences of a searing passion, ecstatic sex?

Ritual

If a man has not committed too grave a crime it is not impossible to love himself back into his wife's arms. It is even easy to do this, if she is sick, weary, or weak in some way. Langley, when we left the mountains, was all of these things. My behavior with our daughters exasperated her. My assumption that Susannah was pure and Magdalena a tramp. She had left the home and social circle that she knew in Long Island to follow our shared anthropological star to Mexico. There she had dutifully masqueraded as a pastor's wife. And even gaily lived in sin, after I elevated myself to priest. She had, being Langley, gone beyond this role to become a sunny and welcomed force among the village women, making friends she cherished and busily writing down every aspect of their ways.

Her sacrifice was in the isolation she endured, far from her family and friends; the absence of a daily newspaper, the *Times*; the remoteness of our splendid wilderness in the thin air that we loved.

My own remorse for having struck the child was great. In the solitude of my ostracism, an estrangement from all my girls, Langley as well as June and Susannah, I contemplated my error. I could find no justification for it. Yes, the child was willful, disobedient. She was born that way. The idea that a child comes into the world a clean slate is a ridiculous one. When she was two and we tried out the notion of shoes on her feet, she rebelled. At five she said a final no, thank you to oatmeal. At six she wanted a zipper at the front of her pants just like I had. And then the red zippered pants Langley had found for her caused offense. In her child's mind—but after how many previous lifetimes as a discriminating being! my friends the Mundo shamans might say—they did not seem serious enough. After all, I never wore red trousers.

I prayed over it. Spare the rod, spoil the child. One says that and swallows down one's immediate protest. Stifles the voice that hates the rod. Would never, on its own, have even thought about the rod. There was something in me, I found, that followed ideas, beliefs, edicts, that had been put into practice, into motion, before I was born.

And this "something" was like an internalized voice, a voice that drowned out my own. Beside which, indeed, my own voice began to seem feeble. Submissive. And when I allowed myself to think about that submission I thought of myself as having been spiritually neutered. And thought, as well, of the way Langley, Magdalena, and even the all-accepting Susannah sometimes looked at me. In dismay and disappointment. Daddy, the girls seemed to ask, where is your own spark? Langley seemed resigned to the fact that it was missing.

How long it took me to realize it was the *me*ness of me that was missing! That next to the men of the Mundo village, even before we could comfortably converse with them, I was a shadow. It wasn't, as I used to think, that I wore the long black coat and black hat and trousers that marked my occupation as shepherd of souls, no. In some odd way I was, the self of me, canceled out. I was a man mouthing words that sparkled, but going through the motions of my own life.

Except, in our most private life, with Langley. There was grounding in her presence. In her arms. Grounding especially in her laughter, the naked shedding of roles that was her sleep. I loved even to hear her snore, though to awaken and see me peering at her as she did so embarrassed her. Then she would grab a pillow and jam it over her head. And I would tug it off, and tussle with her. Her warm naked body the fire of life. Her breath the breathing of life. And when she was sick and weary and weak, and when she cried in frustration or when she was angry enough at me to throw chairs—then it seemed to me I loved her so much I was in danger of forgetting the voice inside my head, forgetting even the voice I began to recognize as "God's."

We had agreed, even before we were married, that we would never lay a hand on our child. We believed in correction, which we thought could be accomplished by reason and consistency; we did not believe in corporal punishment. This had been of such importance to us that we had discussed it thoroughly, over years, until Langley felt it was safe for her to bear a child. By beating her eldest daughter, to the point of actually drawing blood, caused by the disks on the accursed belt I used, I had betrayed her completely.

We were beaten in slavery! she screamed, weeping as if her heart would break.

She cried every night and would not let me enter the big bedroom with the gauze curtains that blew limply in the muggy summer heat.

And each night, as soon as the girls were asleep, I made my way there, to her door. On my knees, outside the locked door, I pleaded.

Only forgive me, I said. I do not expect, or deserve, anything more. Please do not cry, I said. Crying now, myself. I am not worth one tear that falls from your beautiful eyes.

Don't break any more of your precious treasures, I said. As a crystal vase we'd kept in storage while in Mexico—a vase she loved—crashed against the door.

Everything in me wanted to break down the door, pin her flailing arms to her sides, drag her to the bed, lick away every tear, drink from her flowing body, and pour my whole being into hers. But I, my heart breaking, could not rise from my knees. She had seen me turn into a monster; how could I ever expect her to forget? I fell asleep there, growing cramped and chilled as the night wore on.

In the morning, her face wrinkled as a crone's and tear-stained, she opened the door, sniffed at me as if I were disagreeable garbage, and stepped gingerly around my cold, ashen, and yellowing feet.

This nightly ritual seemed to go on forever. During the day I called June June. I took her and Susannah to the YWCA, where they swam and made macramé wall hangings. I took them shopping. I went to Montauk with them, where an old friend of mine had the very last house before the Island petered out into the sea. In the nonexistent traffic there, I taught June to drive.

Preoccupied, I tried to imagine my life without Langley. I could not. For without Langley all of it was just going through the motions, following the dictate of the voice in my ear, the emptiness in my soul. But there was no warmth without her, no fire. No rebellion of my own angel to enjoy. No surprise.

She became so weak from her grief that when she stepped over me in the mornings, she stumbled. She was eating next to nothing. I was the same. I think we both had fevers, for our nightly exertions took their toll.

I begged her to let me take care of her. She laughed, a mean laugh. And tossed her hair, which since our return from Mexico she'd both straightened and bobbed. In her plum-colored silk pajamas and fluffy-toed mules she was a different woman—which I found amazing and almost unbearably exciting. She had also begun taking courses in comparative anthropology at the local college. It drove me crazy not to be making love to her and, while loving her, learning her new thoughts.

I decided to learn golf.

It did not work. I disliked the cap. The cart. The balls. And hadn't I heard somewhere that the green itself, because of the chemicals used to keep it so, was toxic?

One morning she did not leave her room. By then I had dragged my mattress from my room and slept on it just beside her door. After half an hour of waiting, I went inside. Surprised to find that the door was not locked. She could not get out of bed. Seeing this, I felt—it is almost impossible to describe, except to say I felt the mother in me fully ripen and rise to the occasion. Suddenly I was all over the room at once, tending to Langley; changing the sheets, opening the windows, adjusting the curtains, picking up newspapers and books from the floor. Then, down in the kitchen, I made soup, squeezed oranges, made toast. Got the children out of the house. Then I came back, watched Langley eat, tucked her in, and went to my room to dress.

During the day I looked in on her. Fed her. Went to the market for anything she said she had a hankering for—the father in me loving the activity of sallying forth! And in the evening I dragged out all the records we'd stored in her parents' basement before we went to Mexico, the records to which we'd danced before the voice in my head got the better of me, and I lit a candle, only one because it was so hot, and Langley had by now reverted to the woman I knew. The heat had made her hair go back to its naughty kinkiness, and perspiration had ruined the silk pajamas, and she didn't know where the mules were, and she loved being naked anyhow.

And now I waited. I was waiting to see in Langley's brown eyes, which sometimes looked maroon, if she still wanted me, old man, sinner, beast, creature that I was. If she remembered how it felt to be with me. To be pinned to the bed by me. To be herself riding me. Did she think of the taste of me, which she said she loved, or remember the feeling of me tasting her, my tongue eager and intent as a spaniel's? Or did she remember how hot nights made loving even better because bodies stuck together? And there was more noise and slipperiness and more moisture of all kinds to absorb. And did she remember my telling her, when we made love, and she gave herself completely to me, *Baby I love you and Baby I love you is the most erotic thing I know?*

Naked, nappy, bright-eyed, and almost well, she began to study me. I felt it immediately. She did it when my back was turned. On my way to the kitchen. Out the door to the store. Bending to retrieve the spoon she'd dropped. The one she'd licked long and suggestively with her rapidly recovering tongue.

She caught me watching, and laughed. You have a tongue fetish, she said.

© VACHELLE

ALICE WALKER won the Pulitzer Prize and the National Book Award for her novel *The Color Purple*. Her many other bestselling books include *Possessing the Secret of Joy* and *The Temple of My Familiar*. She is the author of five novels, two collections of short stories, three collections of essays, five volumes of poetry, and several children's books. Her books have been translated into more than two dozen languages. Born in Georgia, Alice Walker now lives in Northern California.

FINAL VINYL DAYS

Jill McCorkle

Dear BRC Reader,

Jill McCorkle has been called our contemporary Eudora Welty. She tames the outrageous, humanizes the forbidden, and grounds the hilarious. *Final Vinyl Days* is nine fabulous new short stories, all of them about characters traveling off the beaten path. "Final Vinyl Days" is about a guy who graduated (some time ago) with a 3.7 in English Lit and who means to keep clerking in a vintage shop forever. "It's A Funeral! RSVP" is about a woman who plans what she calls Going-Out Parties—her clients aren't the "survivors"; they are the soon-to-be deceased themselves. Or listen to the narrator of "The Anatomy of Man"—a young pastor who hears voices while relaxing (off-hours) in the heated baptismal pool. Then there is "Your Husband Is Cheating on Us," a selection from which follows.

Leona Nevler
Senior Vice President
and Editorial Director

Your Husband Is Cheating on Us

Your husband is cheating on us. I'm assuming that he hasn't told you yet. I'm the test wife and he tries everything out on me first, I mean *everything*. Remember when he got hooked on that massage oil that heats up with body temp? Now maybe you liked it, but I sure didn't. I got a rash, but of course, I have extremely sensitive skin and always have. I mean, I am Clinique all the way. If you were writing up this triangle (fast becoming a rectangle), then *you'd* be the one with sensitive skin, the fair, hothouse flower, and I'd be the scrub grass by the side of the road.

And look at you—some tan. I know that you go to Total Skin Care and get in the sunning beds. It's odd how he tells me all about you. There have been many times when I've said, well, why don't you just go on home then? And of course, that's the ironic part, because he always does. But, girl, like are you thick? I would *know* if my man had been out messing around. Like I know your perfume—Chloe—and the fact that you have not picked up on my Shalimar is amazing. I wear the stuff the way it's supposed to be worn—heavy; I'm one of those women people ask not to be seated next to on the airplane. At my last clerical job they ran a ban on perfume in the workplace after I'd been there a week, so I had to quit on principle. That's me, a quitter; a principled quitter. When the going gets tough I get the hell out, always have.

I've come here today with a proposition for you, but before I get into that, I thought you might like to hear a bit about me. I'd think you'd want to, given that I know everything there is to know about you. I know your mama died last January, and I have to tell you that I almost called you up to give my condolences. I mean, I'd been hearing about how awful her illness was and how you were traveling back and forth to tend to her. I heard you on the answering machine many times when I'd be over here cooking dinner. I've got to tell you that I just love your kitchen—that commercial-size stove and those marble countertops. Was he feeling guilty when you all remodeled, or what? You and I both have excellent and very similar tastes. Don't look at my hair. It's not a good day. You should see me when it's just cut and blown dry. Maybe I can show you some time.

Anyway, one of those nights when I heard you on the machine, you were crying so hard that I almost picked up, so strong was my urge to want to comfort you. When Mr. Big got home, I told him there was a message I felt he had to listen to right that minute, and of course, he did, but then did he call you? No, ma'am. And did he call to check on your son, who he had dumped off at the Anderson house and them not even home from work yet? I told him that if I had a son I believe I'd be more responsible with him, and he just pawed the air like I might be dumb. He must do that to you a lot, too. I'm sure he must. I even suggested I excuse myself, go to the mall or something so he could have his privacy but he just waved again and shrugged, like, ayyhh. Well, that was the first time I stopped and asked myself just who in the hell was this man I was sharing my (or *your*) bed with? I looked at him in a completely different way after that. I mean, how could he hear you sobbing and carrying on like that and not rush to call you? I see your surprise and I'm sorry. We all grow up and find out that the truth hurts. But here's some truth you might like. I did *not* sleep with him in your bed that night. I faked myself a migraine (complete with blinding aura) and made him drive me straight home. Do you think *he* ever looked all around to make sure your neighbors weren't looking? Hell, no. Either too stupid or just didn't give a damn, I can't figure which. I moaned and groaned and talked of the bright lights I was seeing out of my right eye (I told him the left had already shut out in complete blindness), and honey, he drove faster than the speed of light. I have always noticed how men (at least the ones I've come into contact with) can't stand to observe pain. It just sends them right up a tree. I have also faked menstrual cramps with Mr. Big on several occasions, and so I know in great detail (he talks a hell of a lot, doesn't he?) that you have just terrible periods and always have. My bet is that you've faked your share, am I right? Well, either way, I know how you sometimes ask him to crush up some Valium into some juice that you sip through a straw so you don't have to sit up and straighten yourself out. Genius. Make that Mr. Big Ass work! But honey, I'm not so sure I'd trust him, you know? If I were you I might mix my own cocktails.

But enough about that, I wanted to tell you about me. Get yourself a drink if you like, or a cigarette. I know you smoke. He knows you smoke, even though you think he doesn't. I mean, the man is slow for sure, but he isn't completely out of the loop. He has smelled it in your hair, even though he says you spray lots of hairspray and perfume (*he* doesn't know you wear Chloe—I do). So come on out in the open and just smoke. I smoked for years and I absolutely loved it. But I quit years ago. I am actually one of those who quit because of Yul Brynner coming on television and saying that, when I saw him there doing that ad, then it meant he was dead. Lord. That was a moving experience. I was holding a cigarette in my hand and was seven months pregnant (yes I have had a life, too), and I felt like Yul was looking directly into my eyes. Talk about an aura. Yul had an aura, and don't be like Mr. Big and make a joke about his baldness. I felt his soul reach out and grab me by the throat and say, *Put out the butt.* I went out on my back stoop, took one final drag (a long, delicious drag), and then I thumped that butt clean across the darkened backyard where it twinkled and glowed for just a brief second before dying.

If I was somebody who could like have one cookie at a time or could eat the designated portion written at the top of the recipe or on the side of the box, then I'd ask you to give me a cigarette, but we know better. If I had one cigarette, I'd have a carton. I have always told people that if I was ever given the bad news that my number had been drawn in that great bingo game we call fate and I only had a little bit of time left, that I'd get me a cooler of beer and a carton of cigarettes and several bottles of Hawaiian Tropic (the oil with the red label for tropical-looking people), a tape deck with all my favorites from when I was a teenager: Pet Clark and Chad and Jeremy, you know my time, I'm a few years older than you, I think. And I'd just stretch out and offer myself to the sun; a burnt offering. Burnt, greased, and buzzing like a bee.

The baby? You're asking about *my* baby? Well, let's just say that if I had a baby then my last wish would be a very different one. But that's not something I like to talk about. I'll tell you what I did come to talk about. You see, I have been thinking that we should get rid of Mr. Big. That's right, don't look so shocked until you hear me out. It would be just like in that movie that came out a year or two ago, only I do not want to get into a lesbian entanglement with you. I mean, no offense or anything, it's just not my cup of tea. Actually I would like some of whatever you're drinking. Diet Coke is fine. Don't slip me a Mickey, okay? A joke, honey. That's a joke. I'm full of them. Probably every joke you've heard over the past eight years has been right from my mouth. Mr. Big has no sense of rhythm or timing—in *anything*, you know?

Truth is you look a far sight better than how he painted you, and you look a damn lot better than that photo of you all in that church family book. I mean it made me sick to see Mr. Big Ass sitting there grinning like he was the best husband in the world when of course I knew the truth. Honey, there are facts and then there are facts, and the fact is that he is a loser with a capital *L*.

Arsenic is big where I'm from. I guess anywhere you've got a lot of pests there's a need for poison, and then maybe your perception of what constitutes a pest grows and changes over the years. There was a woman from a couple of towns over who went on a tear and fed arsenic to practically everybody she knew. If she had had herself a religious mission like Bo and Peep or Do and Mi, whatever those fools were called who tried to hitch a ride on the comet by committing suicide in new Nikes, or like that Waco freak, or, you know, that Jim guy with the Kool-Aid down in Guyana, she'd have gotten a lot of coverage—*People* magazine, *Prime Time*, you name it. When they finally wised up to her, she had enough ant killer stashed in her pantry to wipe out this whole county. It's big in this state. Cyanide, too, might be good because you've got that whiff of almond you might could hide in some baked goods. But I don't know how to get that.

I know what you're thinking, sister. I've been there. You see, your husband has been faithful to me for eight long years, and why he up and pulled this stunt I don't know. Middle-age crazy, I suspect. Maybe he wanted somebody younger and shapelier. Maybe he wanted somebody a little more hot to trot like my oldest friend—practically a relative—who sleeps with anybody who can fog a mirror, and her own little lambs fast asleep in the very next room

If I had had my own little lamb, my life would have been very different. And I was going to tell you about the real me, so I'll just begin before I go back to my plan. You keep thinking about it while I do my autobiography for you. You see, I think that my first knowledge that I would live the life I do is when I was in the eighth grade and my foot jumped right into a size nine shoe. Now I'm looking over and I see that you are about a seven and a half, which is a very safe place for a foot to be these days. That's a safe size. But I hit nine so fast and all of the women in my family said, "Where did she get that foot?" My brother called me Big Foot. My great-aunt said, "Oh my God in heaven, what if she grows into those?" This from a woman who was so wide, her butt took up a whole shopping aisle at the CVS. I mean, it isn't exactly like I came from aristocracy but they thought so, or at least they thought that a slim little petite foot meant that somebody way, way back stepped off the boat in some size fours.

I maxed out at a size ten when I was a senior in high school. There they are, full-grown pups, and honey, there isn't a single shoe on the market that I don't order and wear. Sometimes I have to order a ten and a half (I firmly believe that this is the result of the Asian influence in this country). I finally got to an age where I could look out at the world and say, "Fine—I am of good solid peasant stock; I am earth woman, working the fields, turning the soil." I can dig with my hands, and I can dig with my feet. My folks aren't sitting out on the veranda as much as they'd like to be. They are picking cotton and to-bacco leaves, and when they get their tired hot bodies back to the shanties at the edge of the field, then here comes The Mister from the Big House. I know that might sound stupid to you, but the size of my feet made me both tough and subservient. I thought long ago that it could all turn around with me meeting the right person at the right time, but that has yet to happen.

You know when I first met Mr. Big, though, I thought it might be happening. Part of the reason I liked him so much that first time is be-cause he talked a lot about you and your son, and he really did seem to care. I even asked him the first time we met in a more personal way, you know, didn't it bother him that he was cheating on you. He said at the time that it was okay because you were cheating on him; I let it be an excuse because he did look pretty cute back then, but I think I knew that you weren't really having an affair. I mean, you had a one-year-old. Now, I've never had a one-year-old but I sure do read enough, and know enough folks who do, that I know the odds of you having time to run around were out of the question. You were proba-bly lucky to get a shower, am I right?

He showed me a picture of your son the first night I ever met him—a cute little thing, plump and grinning—but after we started sleeping together he never showed me any more pictures of your boy. Or you for that matter, other than Mr. Big's Holier Than Thou Church Photo. I should have known to leave him alone right then. I should have said *kiss off* and disappeared. And I'm still not entirely sure why I stayed, except that I was very lonely and I knew that he was safe.

I'm still lonely. I know you might think I'm putting too much stock on the size of my feet, but in my mind it is a physical symbol of my difference in my family. They are all over there in the nice warm room lit by firelight, and I'm way off yonder by the barbed-wire fence with snow on my boots while I shiver and peep in. I've always felt that way, and therefore I'm comfortable with it. I used to get hopeful every now and then, but I got over it.

And this woman! She is much younger than you are, honey. And she has got boobs such that you could place a cafeteria tray there (man-made, I'm sure). Short skirts. Over the knee boots, I mean, really. Everybody says I have awful taste in clothes, and I do much better than she does. I mean to tell you Mr. Big has hit bottom. Here he had us, two perfectly good-hearted, good-looking women, and he falls for *that*? If I were you, I might even take precautions against disease. She might be packaged to look clean, but that is one sordid thing. Check her out some time. I have her working schedule at Blockbuster's, and I know her address and phone number. As a matter of fact I've already started in harassing her for you. Don't thank me. I'm doing it for me, too.

So, I say we bump him off. Real easy. Slip him the poison. Start in small doses and then up it and up it until he's so sick with what seems to be the flu or some awful stomach problem and then we either choke or smother him, say he did it while trying to be a pig and eat while you weren't around. If you carry it through, you know, fall completely apart—grieve, rage, mention that hussy whore girlfriend down at Blockbuster, don't tamper with the will (a document that does not make a single mention of me!), then they'll believe you. Then just say that you feel you've got to get that man in the ground as quickly as possible.

Done. Then you go on about your business and I go on about mine and they might put Miss Blockbuster in the slammer. Truth is that I don't have much business and never have.

I almost had a baby one time. The daddy was nowhere to be found. Get up and shake the sheets, and he'd blown clean out the window and down the road, never to be heard from again. Well, here came a baby. Everybody kept telling me to get rid of it, but when have I *ever* done what anybody said to me? Never. So I plodded along, planning. I had lots and lots of plans. But it was a bad joke—a fake baby. No breath, no heartbeat. I looked at it and realized that was my life. No breath, no heartbeat. No life for me. I'm a slave girl—a servant. I'm one rung lower than a dog.

Mr. Big is too low to be called a dog; that would be an insult to canines everywhere. He didn't call you back that time. He was never there for me, not that I ever expected it; but what if just once he had been? What if just once somebody had taken better care of me, taken me to a real doctor, gotten some help. And Mr. Big knows that you've been feeling down lately, but does Mr. Big care? No. I say we kill him.

Oh, but I see doubt in your eyes. I see love, and for that I sure am sorry for you. You better lose that light, honey.

Bring him down. Think of Delilah. Cut off his strength and watch him go blind and pull a building down on himself. Sap him while you can.

Oh, my, stop crying. Lord. I didn't come over here for this. You are not the woman I thought you were from that photo in the church book. You looked to me in that picture like a woman who could enlist in a complicated plot, but you are a bundle of jumpy weepy nerves. I know that we'd no sooner put Mr. Big down under, but what you'd be confessing and giving out my name. You are a tattletale. You were probably one in school and you're still one. I still call and hang up on the tattletale from my school, that's how much I hate a tattletale.

Oh, yeah, I can see it all, now. You're sitting there thinking about how you could nail *me*. The wife would get it easy. A woman under stress conned by the mistress. You're crazy if you think I'd fall for that one. I may not have any children to worry over, but I have pride. I have dignity. I have the child I almost had and lots of times that keeps me in line. I imagine where he'd be right now, twelve years old—my son waiting for me to get home so he can complain about what I don't have in the refrigerator. I tell people, maybe men I might've just met, "Oh no, I don't stay out late. My son will be waiting for me." Don't think I don't know what it feels like. I was pregnant. I had mood swings. I studied all those wonderful little pictures of the fishy-looking baby growing legs like a tadpole—moving from water to land, just that easily.

But you have everything for real. You have Mr. Big legally.

You are hopeless, woman. I'm the one that ought to be crying! Snap to. Listen to some good advice, because in a minute I'll be out of here. You tell him that you know all about that little bitch he's been seeing (she works at Blockbuster Video and wears way too much eye makeup). Tell him he better shape his butt up or you are out of here, sister. Make him sweat. I mean I don't want a thing to do with him, you know? So use me. Call me by name. Tell him I'll come to your divorce hearing and help you clean up. Get him back if you want him, and make him behave. But don't let him off easy. Pitch a blue blazing fit. Scream, curse, throw things. Let him have it, honey. Your husband is cheating on us. Let him have it. And when all is said and done, please just forget that I was ever here; that I ever walked the earth. After all, I'm Big Foot. Who knows if I even exist.

© MICHAEL MUNDY

JILL McCORKLE's first collection of stories, *Crash Diet* (1992), which *Fortune* called "a perfect little book," was named by both *The New York Times Book Review* and *The Atlanta Journal–Constitution* as one of the year's best books. She is also the author of five novels and has taught writing at the University of North Carolina, Bennington College, Tufts University, and Harvard. A native of Lumberton, North Carolina, she lives now in Massachusetts with her husband and two children.

MISTLER'S EXIT

Louis Begley

Dear BRC Reader,

Louis Begley, who has a fulltime career as an attorney, began to write in mid-life and in seven years has published five brilliant novels. His latest is *Mistler's Exit*.

Thomas Mistler has always thought himself "a happy man, as the world goes." A scion of old money, he made his own fortune in advertising and is now poised to sell the company he founded for a fabulous price. But when a medical examination reveals the presence in his liver of a fatal intruder, "preposterously, unmistakably, he begins to rejoice," with a feeling of having been set free. Without revealing his illness to his family, he sets out for Venice, his favorite city in the world. The novel is about what happens to him there.

Leona Nevler
Senior Vice-President
and Editorial Director

Pushing his luggage cart along the airport building to the jetty, where water taxis dock, he began to feel lightheaded, as though he had been puffing too long on a cigar that bled. Had he begun to resemble his mother and certain old ladies of her acquaintance, always on the lookout, like border police, for twinges of pain, swellings, and eruptions of the skin not identified before? Otherwise, why was it so urgent to know whether this mixture of fatigue and nausea was a genuinely new feature in the landscape of his existence? Since the conversations with the doctors, he had begun to wish for an hourglass that would show, moment by moment, the ebbing of his strength. Probably, no instrument existed sensitive enough to distinguish the effect of a night on the plane, and the wait at Roissy for the connection, from the goings-on in that deviant and numb organ inside him, but at least some of the feeling that he was unable to take another step had to be a message it was sending. Mistler steadied himself against the railing, closed his eyes, then opened them to stare at the water. The luggage cart was no friend. Had he called for a porter he might have leaned on his arm, however indelicate the gesture. Taking a deep breath, to clean his mouth, lungs, and brain, he asked the dispatcher to get him a taxi.

A light mist clung to the surface of the lagoon. Mistler stood in the aft, incurious and excited, waiting for the islands to appear. The spray cooled his face. He lit a cigar to cover the taste of his saliva and quickly threw it away. Had Clara been with him, he might have held her hand. She always had chewing gum or mints in her handbag. Would it have been better to bring her? This trip, the white lie he had told, the longing to find something he couldn't quite define, were they some sort of bet? In that case, he was on both sides of it. What could he expect from any action? In a few weeks or months, when the greater unpleasantness began, he would see this holiday for what it was—an expensive farce paid for in unfamiliar units of strength that no amount of rest or sleep could renew. Was it then that he would finally learn it was no use always sailing so close to the wind, determined to stay on course, obsessed by the effort? They entered the channel. The boatman opened the throttle, leaving a wake like a fan of white feathers. Here and there, solitary dinghies swayed on anchor. Men fishing for eel? The sun was in Mistler's eyes. He put on his dark glasses, and, as though the gesture had magic properties, the tower of Madonna dell'Orto, the Fondamente Nuove, became visible, gathered volume. San Michele was before them. The boat slowed down. Mistler recognized successively the shapes of Santa Maria della Misericordia and the Gesuiti, the entrance to the Arsenal. He would have liked to stop the boat altogether, to have the shoreline remain in place for a moment, to take in the city more strongly. But it required too great an effort to go forward through the cabin to speak to the boatman and deal with his bewilderment at a request not included in the fare. He settled for looking hard. Facades of palaces appeared mysteriously and disappeared as the boat threaded its way through the lateral canals. They passed the Hotel Metropole. San Giorgio was before them, dead ahead. As they turned toward the mouth of the Grand Canal, the Dogana and the Salute appeared. Shimmering of blue, gold, and white. The boat went into reverse, a man who had spent his life doing just that caught the line the boatman threw him and made it fast. For the first time in his life feeling something that might be considered. Mistler stepped ashore and entered the lobby of the hotel.

Signor Anselmo, the chief concierge, and his assistant, both of whom Mistler considered, depending on his mood, either friends or a species of questionable investments, rather like tax shelters that returned no income but made unending calls for cash, came forward, in their haste upstaging the assistant manager.

La signora is already here, murmured Signor Anselmo.

Was the man mad? Did he not recognize him? What was he mumbling about? Clara had called just before he left for the airport, saying she was in San Francisco. If this were some sort of a 1940s movie stunt, she might, of course, in reality have been telephoning from Kennedy and taken an Alitalia plane to Milan, in which case she would have beaten his own flight via Paris and gotten to Venice first. He had never known her to like flashy surprises or practical jokes. As practical jokes went, this one, however well intentioned, would be unwelcome; infuriating wouldn't be too strong. He didn't have enough time to be patient, let alone amused, by people's crossing his plans. Of course, she didn't know that.

La signora brought flowers and left her luggage downstairs. Shall I have it taken up?

Certainly, with my bags. I need them right away.

Welcome to your home in Venice, Mr. Mistler. You have your usual apartment. That was the assistant manager.

Thank you. Then there is no need to accompany me. I'll just take the key.

La signora took it.

Then please give me the double.

He waved away the hand that would have relieved him of his briefcase. His address book was inside it. Very early morning in New York, perfect time to catch people at home, some of them before they got out of bed. No matter how he felt, this was the time for his telephone calls. The elevator stopped at the second floor. He followed the blood-red carpet to the double door at the end of the corridor, and opened it. A raincoat hung in the little foyer. Not Clara's. The two enormous windows of the sitting room that gave on the canal were open; "I've Got You Under My Skin," whistled with weird accuracy, could be heard from the other room, which was on the right. The door was ajar. Clara didn't whistle; she sang her Cole Porter repertory off-key. Mistler put his briefcase on the sofa, knocked, and, without waiting for an answer, walked in. It was, after all, his suite. On the bed, wearing a white terrycloth peignoir marked with the hotel's insignia, sat Lina Verano. She was drying her toes, one by one, with a small hand towel.

Mr. Mistler! She stood up. Her hair was wet, and hung in strands on her perfectly smooth cheeks. She was prettier than he had found her at Anna's, but in the strong daylight seemed less juvenile.

Please excuse me. Your plane must have been early. I didn't think you would be here for another hour, so I took a bath. I would have put everything back so you wouldn't have ever noticed. Look, I brought you all of these.

She pointed. There were roses and peonies—white, red, and pink—on the dressing table in the bedroom and on the coffee table and marble-topped gueridons in the sitting room.

Aren't they beautiful? Say something, Mr. Mistler!

Only one thing comes to mind: What are you doing in my hotel room?

Someone, presumably the porter, was pounding on the outside door. Mistler shouted, *Avanti!* His luggage. A moment later, the porter reappeared, pulling behind him a gray suitcase on wheels like a mutt on a leash. Mistler tipped him, and waited while the man disposed of the stuff in the bedroom.

I repeat, what are you doing here?

You knew I was coming to see you in Venice. You said it was all right. I couldn't find a room in any of the *pensioni* I know, so I came here, just to meet you. I left my suitcase downstairs. I am sorry I used your bathroom. I guess I didn't read you as well as I thought. I sort of thought you might be glad to see me. Amused. Who knows?

And what was my wife going to say?

I knew she wasn't coming! I called the hotel the day after Mrs. Williams's party to make sure you were staying here, and they said the reservation was for you alone. Then, to make sure, I also checked the airline. Do you mind so very much? I can leave right away. If I find a place to stay, I'll call you tomorrow. I may have to try a hotel in Mestre. They're less expensive.

Good Lord, said Mistler. You can't walk out of here dressed like this. They'd take the peignoir from you at the front desk, and I hate to think of the riot that would follow. Look, give me fifteen minutes. I'm very tired and I have some telephone calls to make.

I am so sorry. I can stay in the bedroom while you telephone.

She knelt down beside the dreadful suitcase, took a book from it, and told him she wouldn't mind if he closed the door.

LOUIS BEGLEY was born in Poland and came to the United States with his parents, who were refugees from the Nazis. He is a graduate of Harvard College and Harvard Law School and practices in New York. His first novel written in mid-life, *Wartime Lies,* was winner of the PEN Hemingway Award and *The Irish Times* Book Prize. It was nominated for the National Book Award, the National Book Critics Award, and *The Los Angeles Times* Book Prize. His most recent novel, *About Schmidt,* was a National Book Critics Circle Award nominee as well. He has quickly become a major literary figure.

CRUEL AS THE GRAVE

Sharon Kay Penman

Dear BRC Reader,

Cruel as the Grave marks the return of Sharon Kay Penman to the Ballantine list. The continuation of Penman's series that was launched with the Edgar Award-nominated *The Queen's Man*, this new historical novel, set in twelfth-century England, reunites Eleanor of Aquitaine and her resourceful detective/special agent Justin de Quincy.

Once again, de Quincy adopts his role as "the queen's man," working on behalf of Eleanor in her search for her missing son, Richard Lionheart. And once again, de Quincy's role embraces the investigation of murder.

Melding historical authenticity with the pulsating cadence of a thriller, Sharon Kay Penman's *Cruel as the Grave* is "masterfully told. [Her] authentic period details, larger-than-life characters, and fast-paced plot add up to great reading for both mystery fans and mystery buffs."*

Joe Blades
Associate Publisher

*Booklist

Tower of London
England

April 1193

They were intimate enemies, bound by blood. Here in the torchlit splendor of the Chapel of St John the Evangelist, they'd fought yet another of their battles. As always, there was no winner. They'd inflicted wounds that would be slow to heal, and that, too, was familiar. Nothing had changed, nothing had been resolved. But never had the stakes been so high. It shimmered in the shadows between them, the ultimate icon of power: England's royal crown.

Few knew better than Eleanor of Aquitaine how seductive that power could be. In her youth, she'd wed the French king, then left him for the man who would become King of England. That passionate, turbulent marriage of love and hate was part of her distant, eventful past; if Henry's unquiet ghost still stalked the realm of marital memory, she alone knew it. Now in her seventy-first year, she was England's revered Dowager Queen, rising above the ruins of her life like a castle impervious to assault. If her fabled beauty had faded, her wit had not, and her will was as finely honed as the sword of her most celebrated son, Richard Lionheart, the crusader king languishing in a German prison. But she was much more than Richard's mother, his invincible ally: She was his only hope.

The torches sputtered in their wall sconces, sending up wavering fingers of flame. The silence grew louder by the moment, thudding in her ears like an army's drumbeat. She watched as he paced, this youngest of her eagles. John, Count of Mortain and Earl of Gloucester, would-be king. He seethed with barely suppressed fury, giving off almost as much heat as those erratic torches. His spurs struck white sparks against the tiled floor, and the swirl of his mantle gave her a glimpse of the sword at his hip. This might be her last chance to reach him, to avert calamity. What could she say that he would heed? What threat was likely to work? What promise?

"I will not allow you to steal Richard's crown," she said tautly. "Understand that if you understand nothing else, John. As long as I have breath in my body, I will oppose you in this. As will the justiciars."

"You think so?" he scoffed. "They held fast today, but who knows what may happen on the morrow? They might well decide that England would be better served by a living king than a dead one!"

"Richard is not dead."

"How can you be so sure of that, Madame? Have you second-sight? Or is this merely a doting mother's lapse into maudlin sentimentality?"

Beneath his savage sarcasm, she caught echoes of an emotion he would never acknowledge: a jealousy more bitter than gall. "Bring us back incontrovertible proof of Richard's death," she said, "and we will then consider your claim to the throne."

John's eyes showed sudden glints of green. "You mean you would weigh my claim against Arthur's, do you not?"

"Richard named his nephew as his heir. I did not," she said pointedly. "Must I remind you that you are my son, flesh of my flesh? Why would I not want the kingship for you?"

"That is a question I've often asked myself."

"If you'd have me say it, listen, then. I want you to be king. Not Arthur—you."

He could not hide a flicker of surprise. "You almost sound as if you mean that."

"I do, John," she said. "I swear by all the saints that I do."

For a moment, he hesitated, and she thought she'd gotten to him. But not whilst Brother Richard lives?"

"No," she said, very evenly, "not whilst Richard lives."

The silence that followed seemed endless to her. She'd always found it difficult to read his thoughts, could never see into his soul. He was a stranger in so many ways, this son so unlike Richard. His eyes locked upon hers, with a hawk's unblinking intensity. Whatever